THE MOTHERLAND SAGA

The Epic Novel of Turkey

VOLUME TWO

EMERGENCE

1918-1938

THE MOTHERLAND SAGA

The Epic Novel of Turkey

VOLUME TWO

EMERGENCE

1918-1938

HUGO N. GERSTL

PANGÆA
PUBLISHING GROUP

EMERGENCE: 1918 – 1938
Volume Two - The Motherland Saga
The Epic Novel of Turkey

Copyright © 2019 Hugo N. Gerstl
www.HugoGerstl.com

ISBN 978-1-950134-22-9
Pangæa Publishing Group
www.PangaeaPublishing.com

Cover image: Istanbul twilight © Daniel Boiteau, Dreamstime.com
Inside images: Border © Antsvgdal, Dreamstime.com

Cover design and typesetting by
DesignPeaks@gmail.com

For information contact:

PANGÆA PUBLISHING GROUP
25579 Carmel Knolls Drive
Carmel, CA 93923
Telephone: 831-624-3508/831-649-0668
Fax: 831-649-8007
Email: info@pangaeapublishing.com

To Herb and Sharon Chelner, the "bestest" friends,

to Bob and Perihan Mueller, to Anne Secker,

who read the very first draft of the entire book,

to Lisa and Richard

AND FOR MY LORRAINE –

THE CENTER OF MY UNIVERSE

HUGO N. GERSTL

THE MOTHERLAND SAGA
The Epic Novel of Turkey

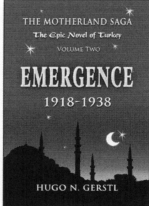
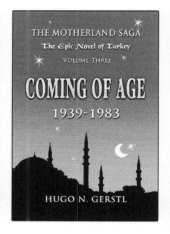

Do not miss them on your shelf!

For Hugo N. Gerstl's complete novels list and descriptions,
go to www.HugoGerstl.com

PANGÆA PUBLISHING GROUP
25579 Carmel Knolls Drive
Carmel, CA 93923
Email: info@pangaeapublishing.com

PROLOGUE

In Volume I, we witnessed the collapse of the five-hundred year-old Ottoman Empire as the First World War, the "War to end all wars," shattered the established order of the civilized world, and presaged the coming of the Twentieth Century.

The futility of war was nowhere better illustrated than in the Battle of Gallipoli where each side entered the battle with half a million men; each side suffered two-hundred-fifty thousand casualties; and at the end, except for the oceans of blood that soaked the earth, and the oceans of tears shed by those left behind, everything remained precisely as it had been a year before, and not one inch of land changed hands.

As we begin this second volume, *EMERGENCE*, the War is grinding down to an end, the Ottoman Empire is collapsing in its death throes, and the Western Powers, having prevailed against the land of the sultans, is preparing to dismember Turkey, carve up and divide the carcass.

But the overwhelming power of the West may be in for surprise ...

PART THREE:

NADJI 1918–1924

1

By the end of 1917, Europe was exhausted. The newly formed Soviet Union had made peace with the Ottoman Empire at Erzinjan. This did not stop the carnage on the frontier. Christians sought revenge for what they perceived as Ottoman bestiality of years gone by. Armenian nationalists massacred hundreds of thousands of Turkish villagers in the east.

Enver Pasha ordered a general offensive to deal with the untenable situation. Turkish forces stormed Erzurum, breaking the Armenian stranglehold in East Anatolia, but the Ottoman Empire could not go on hemorrhaging much longer. By summer, 1918, the mood in Istanbul was grim. It was only a matter of time before the Turkish fronts collapsed.

On June fourteenth, Omer Akdemir, now a two star general, closed the door to his library and addressed his sole surviving son. "Are you sure that's what you want, Nadji? I'm proud you've been accepted into the Turkish Military Academy, but don't you think we've given enough blood to the Empire?"

"Father, we've gone over this again and again. I'm not a little boy, and I'm not Seljuk. I'm sixteen. This is not just a whim."

"But there are several honorable ways to serve your country and not risk your life. Won't you consider the university? After you graduate, if you still want to put in for the academy, you could do so."

"Father, my decision is made. Please realize that and let me go. Besides, no one knows better than you, *Pasha,* it's in our blood."

At slightly over six feet tall, Nadji was three inches taller than his father, with close-cropped light brown hair. He was attractive by any standard. He had the erect bearing of a born soldier. Although Nadji was soft-spoken, he projected an unmistakable aura of leadership, a quiet confidence that charmed rather than overwhelmed. The boy was correct when he said it ran in the blood. The Akdemirs had been a military family for four generations.

Nadji's great grandfather, Hasan Pasha, whose stern visage glared down at the family from a yellowed daguerreotype in the hallway, had been the hero of Sevastopol during the Crimean War in 1855. Grandfather Shefvik had risen to the rank of colonel and would no doubt have become a Pasha, but for his loyalty to the deposed Sultan Abdulaziz.

On his mother's side, great grandfather Lieutenant Bürolü, had been killed at the Battle of Kars, three months before the Paris Peace Conference ended the Crimean War. He left behind an infant son, Grandfather Midhat, who'd retired as a colonel of cavalry in 1900, two years before Nadji's birth.

Nadji's young life had been filled with travel. There were new assignments every few years, as his Father rose higher in the military ranks, and the family accompanied him. When war erupted, Mama assumed command of the family. Nadji had worshipped his brother,

Seljuk, eight years his senior. Seljuk decided early on that he was going to be a general like Father. Nadji determined *he'd* be Seljuk's adjutant. The Akdemir brothers would rise through the ranks together. That dream had been shattered three-and-a-half years ago in the Caucasus, when Seljuk died in battle.

The family had never been the same afterward. Mama often disappeared into her bedroom. Walls were thin. Nadji heard his mother's sobs and his father's fruitless attempts to comfort her. Seljuk's name was not brought up in conversation. The family visited his grave at Istanbul's military cemetery six times each year. Nadji's academic performance and the strong impression he made at his personal interview went a long way toward his selection for early admission to the Turkish Military Academy. His father's rank did not go unnoticed.

"Very well, Nadji, since you speak like a man, I'll address you as one. It's always been a great honor for our family to serve the Ottoman Empire. That empire is dying. I don't know when the final death rattle will come. Perhaps in a month, perhaps in a year, but it will come. In September, you'll enter the academy. Because of our imminent defeat in this war, you may be looked upon with ridicule. What I tell you now is between us. Neither your mother nor your sisters know this. I ask you between father and son – between comrades in arms – to keep what I say within the four walls of this room."

"I shall, Father."

"I accept your word. The Ottoman treasury is bankrupt. There are no more funds available for war. The antiquated weapons we've been using will have to last the duration of the conflict. Last year, we gave up Jerusalem to the British. Now, the entire southern front is collapsing. Mustafa Kemal, the only Turkish general who has never suffered a military defeat in this war, was sent to Syria to shore up our defenses.

He does not believe he can salvage the operation. Do you understand what I'm saying, Nadji?"

The boy nodded. His father continued, "We're trying to obtain the most honorable peace we can. We've been negotiating secretly for over a year, with no progress. That devil Venizelos, who became Greek Premier after King Constantine was expelled, has frustrated our attempts at every turn. That bastard – don't look shocked Son, you'll get used to such language from soldiers soon enough – is smooth as glass. His perfect French and elegant manners have charmed the British and French politicians. The English Prime Minister, Lloyd George, called him 'the greatest Greek politician since Pericles,' while we're portrayed as the 'terrible, bestial Muslim savages who annihilated millions of innocent, *Christian* Armenians and Greeks.

"We can't expect gentle or even 'civilized' treatment from the enemy. You might not even have a military career. The British chargé advised our government that the one non-negotiable point is complete demobilization of the army."

"But father, our family has given officers to our homeland for generations. I wouldn't want to take up any other profession."

"I'm certain you intend to carry on the honor of our name. I'd be less than honest if I didn't advise you of the difficulties you'll face should you choose to accept the appointment to the academy. Having made your decision, I will give you the same advice my father gave me. The Akdemirs are a proud family, harking back to a proud tradition. We respect duty and honor above personal want or ambition. Sometimes it may seem almost impossible in the face of life's trials to adhere to such a practice, which seems outmoded today. But I expect you will live by this heritage, Nadji. Do you understand what I'm saying?"

"I understand, Father, *Sir.*" He smiled. Then the boy's restraint broke. He hugged the older man. "Papa, I made it, *I made it*! I'm going to be an officer after all!"

"May I be the first to salute you, my future Pasha," Omer replied.

"Kerem Effendi, I made it, *I made it*! I'm going to be an officer after all!"

"Indeed, Abbas, and at the top of your class. You have every reason to be proud. You must remember not only your oath as a member of the Internal Security Police. Even more important, you must live by your blood oath to our – inner circle."

"I shall, my friend and teacher." Abbas earnestly repeated the words he'd recited six nights before at a very small, secret meeting. "No matter what, no matter where, I dedicate my existence to the purification of the motherland. To bring the Ottoman Empire back to the days of Süleyman the Lawgiver, we must be ever vigilant, rooting out those foreign elements who pollute and threaten to strangle our Ottoman bloodlines. Jew or Christian, Armenian, Greek or Frenchman, the *yabanji* must be expelled from our homeland like excrement from a human body. I swear by Allah to bring this about, in the name of the Sultan and in the name of our brotherhood."

"Good. Now as my gift to you, you are no longer plain Abbas or even 'Clever Abbas.' You deserve the dignity of two names. Henceforth, you shall be known as Abbas Hükümdar, Abbas the Prince. Even though your first assignment, Stamboul, won't be a very princely precinct in which to begin your labors."

In September, 1918, Nadji Akdemir entered the prestigious Ottoman Military Academy which, despite continuing defeats of Ottoman forces on the battlefield, continued to maintain its proud tradition. His initial training was vigorous. Cadets were up before dawn each morning shining shoes, pressing uniforms, scrubbing down barracks for what was invariably a vicious inspection. Nadji took to sleeping on top of his cot rather than turning down the covers because the time between wakeup and inspection was unmercifully short.

During the first four weeks, the cadet inspector was merciless. As he passed by the row of small, steel beds, the inspector would casually toss a kurush coin on the cover of each. If the coin bounced, well and good. If it didn't, demerits were duly noted. As he searched the area around each cadet's bed, he opened the small closets that held crisply pressed uniforms, starched shirts, and shoes so shiny he could see his reflection in the burnished leather. He'd *better* see his reflection, or there would be more demerits. Occasionally, the point system became ridiculous. One morning, Nadji's neighbor suffered dire misfortune when a fly landed on the pillow of his cot during inspection.

The first year students stifled their laughter as they heard the inspector bawl at his assistant, "Fly on bed, one demerit. Dust on fly, one demerit. Fly not properly squared on the pillow, one demerit. Total, three demerits."

It was not so funny at week's end. Anyone who'd accumulated twenty "down points" during the week was denied weekend leave, and spent what could have been free time painting doorways and cleaning latrines instead. After a month, inspections became easier.

There were ugly rumors in the streets that the hated French general d'Esperey intended to occupy the Ottoman capital. During the third week in October, General Melih, the Academy Commandant, summoned the faculty and cadets to an evening meeting in the main assembly hall. There was nervous shuffling as students sat in full dress wherever they could find a vacant place. The doors closed at eight o'clock.

"Officers, gentlemen," Melih began. "It is my sad duty to advise you that as we speak our diplomatic envoy, General Rauf and Admiral Calthorpe of the British naval forces are negotiating aboard H.M.S. *Agamemnon* for the unconditional surrender of our Ottoman forces. Last week, two of our three Ottoman leaders, Enver Pasha and Jemal Pasha fled Turkey aboard the German warship *Prinz Wilhelm*. Earlier this week, the third member of the triumvirate, Talat Pasha, resigned. General Izzet is now functioning as Grand Vizier." There was an audible gasp in the room. Rumors of the imminent collapse of the war effort had circulated for months, but as time went by and Ottoman forces remained in the field, the populace had developed an immunity to gossip. Now, the unmentionable had come to pass, and the news was coming not from sensationalist newspapers or prophetic doomsayers, but from the top military echelons. "The British have made four concrete demands: the opening of the Dardanelles and Bosphorous, allied occupation of all important strategic points, surrender of Turkish garrisons in occupied territories, and," he hesitated for a moment, before saying, very quietly, "demobilization of the Turkish army."

"What does that mean for our academy, sir?" a senior classman asked.

"For now, nothing," Melih replied. "We'll continue as usual. Cadets are not armed combat soldiers. But we'll be operating on a day-by-day basis. There's little more to say. Prepare yourselves for hard times. May Allah bless our Sultan, and bring peace to his glorious Islamic Empire. You are dismissed."

2

On the last day of October, 1918, Ottoman troops began laying down their arms. At dawn, November 13, Nadji was awakened by a barracks mate. "What is it, Yusuf?" he responded, still half asleep.

"Come with me to Topkapı."

"Are you crazy? Who'd want to go to the old imperial palace today? And why so early?"

"Not the palace, Nadji, the hill overlooking the Bosphorous. We must get there as soon as possible if we want a good view. Don't wear anything that would identify you as military."

"What's this is all about?"

"The 'conquering Allies' are entering Istanbul – they're calling it 'Constantinople' once again – and they're making a big show of it."

"Why would I want to go see that?"

"Suit yourself," Yusuf responded genially. "This place has been deader than a mausoleum, or haven't you noticed? Any excitement at all is better than what we've had around here recently."

"All right," Nadji said. "Give me half an hour.

They arrived at the bluffs above the Bosphorous by nine. Crowds lined the hill. Promptly at ten, fireworks and rockets lit the daytime sky. Over a hundred vessels tooted their horns and whistles, creating a deafening noise as the Allies entered the Ottoman capital. A sixteen-mile-long convoy, from the smallest tug to the largest battleship, churned the waters of the mile-wide strait. The victors arrived in full panoply, with a parade designed to dazzle the populace. British, French, and Italian flags flew in multicolored profusion. But it was the hated blue and white Greek banner that made Nadji's stomach churn.

The two cadets were among the very few Turks who'd turned out for the display. Gülhane Park, adjacent to the old imperial palace, was filled with Greeks, Armenians, Italians, French, and English, who waved small pennants and noisily cheered each new ship that hooted its happy presence. "I wonder where these people would have been had we won the war," Nadji remarked.

"Certainly not here."

"What happens now?"

"More humiliation. Then a long, hard winter."

And more humiliation there was. Two days after Admiral Calthorpe's naval show, General d'Esperey triumphantly led his troops through the ancient Roman gates of Byzantium down Millet Caddesi, past Aya Sofia and the Sultanahmet – the Blue Mosque – to the French headquarters at Topkapı. "Just look at the arrogant bastard!" Yusuf remarked. "Trust the French to rub our noses in dirt with dramatic flair."

"What do you mean, Yusuf? He's riding at the head of his troops on a white horse. That's his prerogative."

"Perhaps," the other man said sourly. "But he's riding without reins. When the Ottomans marched into Istanbul hundreds of years ago, Mehmet the Conqueror, who captured the city in the name of Islam, rode in like that."

Within days, Allies swarmed all over the defeated city. The French set up headquarters in *Stamboul*. The British occupied *Pera*. The Italians had the good grace to move farther up the Bosphorous. Technically, the invaders did not "rule" Constantinople, since Turks theoretically retained political and administrative "control." But to the defeated Muslim majority, it was occupation in all but name. The cadets returned to their classes.

Two successive prime ministers tried unsuccessfully to set up a government. French, British, and, worst of all, the hated Greek forces occupied almost all of southern Turkey.

It was a long, bitter winter. Constantinople, under allied "protection," was listless, fraught with a sense of doom. Coal supplies vanished. The trams did not run. Steamers seldom plied the icy Bosphorous. The main streets were bathed in shadowy light. Side streets were completely dark. No one went out unarmed at night. The few police patrolling the city were corrupt and universally mistrusted. Profiteering was shameless. Turkish money was almost valueless. A loaf of bread, if it could be obtained at all, cost the equivalent of four American dollars.

The Allied command claimed that since Turkish Muslims had slaughtered millions of Christians for no reason whatsoever, they'd lost the right to rule themselves. Since the Allies had won the war, Western civilization was obviously superior to that of the backward Ottomans. Greeks and Armenians continued an endless party for what they termed the "liberating" Allied forces. Christians replaced Muslims in most local government positions. When state schools reopened, only Christians were allowed to attend. Greeks swaggered through the streets of Constantinople, flaunting the blue and white Greek flag. They roughed up any Turk who did not salute it.

In mid-January, a rumor spread like wildfire through Stamboul. "Did you hear, they're installing bells in Aya Sofia? I swear it." A thousand Muslims swarmed up Divan Street to the fifteen-hundred-year-old edifice, which had been a Mosque for the last five centuries, only to find that the rumor was untrue and that the courtyard was still guarded by Turkish troops.

In February, Nadji had a holiday break. His parents' home in Shishli, less than ten miles away from the Academy, was a world apart from the dying old city. Father had put by ample supplies. The house was warmed by coal-fired *mangals*. At dinner on the third day of his stay, father announced, "We have some very special guests coming from Paris tomorrow night."

"Father!" Nadji exclaimed with distaste. "You'd have a foreigner – a Frenchman at that – in our home?"

"Nadji, I'll thank you to keep a civil tongue in your head, until you've listened to what I have to say. Idiots and fools to jump to conclusions. You are neither! The head of our military academy has invited Yujel Orhan, the distinguished Ottoman historian and the only Turkish full professor at the Sorbonne in Paris, to address the school on what it was like to be a Turk living in France during the war. He's bringing his daughter, Halide, with him. I had the privilege of meeting her in the summer of 1915, and I can truthfully say that she is more courageous and has a bigger heart than any officer – I repeat, *any* officer – I've ever commanded. She risked everything to be with her fiancé at Gelibolu. She arrived in time to watch him die the following day. She stayed on and became known as the Angel of Gelibolu. She worked days and nights without sleep in our field infirmary. A thousand men would gladly have given their lives to bring her fiancé back."

"I apologize, Papa," Nadji said quietly. "Please forgive me."

"I do, of course," the general said, smiling warmly. "Your remark never occurred."

Halide instantly captivated the entire family. She brought bottles of rose-petal perfume for the girls, a carved ivory music box for Mama, and a case of the finest Bordeaux wine for the general. Nadji was overwhelmed when he opened his gift, a marble nameplate on which were engraved the words "Nadji Akdemir, Pasha."

Professor Orhan was an elegant man who looked a decade younger than his seventy years. His wife was a slender, attractive woman, with stylish bobbed hair just starting to go gray. He told the Akdemirs that she had been an associate of Karl Feldkirche, a mutual friend of both himself and Omer Akdemir, in Geneva, and that they'd met a few days after General Akdemir and Halide had left Switzerland for Turkey.

Mama covered the large oak dining table with a white, silk tablecloth, hand-painted Kütahya glazed plates, and the family's finest heirloom silver. Dinner was a remarkable change for Nadji, who'd become used to spartan meals at the academy and the numbness of Istanbul. Besides the Orhans, General Akdemir had invited Metin's parents, Doctor and Mrs. Ermenek, and one other guest, a tall, handsome man with electric grey-blue eyes, General Mustafa Kemal, who wore an immaculately-tailored military uniform. As soon as he spotted Halide, his severe face took on a sparkle. "Halide Orhan?"

"It is indeed. My word, Mustafa Kemal *Pasha,* you seem to have moved up in the world. Congratulations, General."

"Thank you, Halide Hanım," he said with a courtly bow. "Unfortunately, there's not much call for Ottoman generals these days. Have you finished your schooling yet?"

"I'm about to graduate from the Sorbonne. I intend to return to Turkey when I do."

"Praise Allah! If we have a hundred like you, we can't help but move forward into the Twentieth Century at last."

Dinner consisted of roast lamb, garden vegetables, and bottles of the hearty red wine Halide had brought from France. After dinner, conversation turned serious. "In Paris, we read only one side of the story," Professor Orhan began, "The newspapers talk about partitioning Turkey. From what I gather, the western powers want to carve it up among themselves until there's nothing left."

"That could actually happen," Doctor Ermenek responded. "We've lost Greece, the Balkans, Palestine, Egypt, and Syria. Most of southeastern Turkey is now in French hands. Armenia got most of the eastern provinces. Italy occupies the southwest. But it's those sons-of-dogs, the Greeks, who concern us most."

"I know what you mean," General Akdemir interjected. "Can you believe that talk about a 'greater Pontic state?' The Greek premier, Venizelos, wants everything from Samsun to Sivas. What's worse, the damned English support his demands."

"That will never happen during my lifetime," Kemal said quietly. "The Turkish people will rise up and throw them all out."

"Do you think we could bring it about?" Halide asked.

"Yes, Halide Hanım," Kemal replied. "The Turks have two things in their favor. They're extraordinarily proud. And they're being bullied by the one enemy they'll fight to the last Turk's death. The Allies will push a little too far." Halide noticed the steely glint in his hard eyes.

"In Paris, they speak highly of Ferid, the new Grand Vizier," Professor Orhan said.

"Droopy Damad," Sayra Ermenek said, drawing derisive laughter. "The Allies' perfect little puppet. No self-respecting Ottoman can imagine him being village constable, let alone Prime Minister of the Empire. He married Abdül Hamid's sister thirty years ago. The sultan sent him to England as a minor diplomat. When he bungled the job after six months, they recalled him to the palace. No one heard of him for the next twenty-five years. When it was time to negotiate the armistice, Mehmet hauled him out of oblivion to be chief of mission. Even parliament wasn't stupid enough to accredit him, so the fool went back to the palace again."

"One must admit," her husband said, "Ferid fulfills the western idea of the 'typical Turkish gentleman.' He dresses like an Englishman of twenty years ago. He's got enough Western 'culture' to talk a good game, and he's got that polite, pompous air they all love to see."

"As far as Turkey's concerned, he's not worth one of these," Kemal said, disdainfully plucking a fig from a nearby fruit bowl.

"Enough!" their hostess interrupted. "It's my son's birthday tomorrow. I've a lovely Viennese-style torte and the finest aperitifs you'll find in what's left of the Ottoman Empire." She clapped her hands. Her two daughters brought out a large marzipan torte with eighteen candles alight.

"Excuse me, Madame Akdemir," Halide said. "Yesterday you told me Nadji was going to be seventeen years old. Why are there eighteen candles on his cake?"

"Different way of counting," she replied. "In the west, the first 'birthday' commemorates the first *anniversary* of birth. In Turkey, they use the far more sensible system of using the actual day of birth as the 'first birthday.'"

The party toasted Nadji, who thanked them. Then they toasted the future of their Motherland.

3

After the auditorium had emptied, Nadji approached Halide. "Your father was magnificent!" he said.

"Thank you, Nadji. Since we're so close to the heart of Istanbul, I wonder if you might show me around the city."

"I don't think you'd want to see it now. It's not the Istanbul you saw when you were here before."

"That's exactly why I want to see it. Sometimes you have to build from the ground up – start all over again. The result can be beautiful."

"There aren't many physical changes in the city. The tourist attractions are still standing, but they're controlled by Greeks and Armenians. The commandant posted strict orders we're not to be in Stamboul after sunset unless absolutely necessary. Even then, we're to make certain there are no less than three of us together at the same time."

"Nadji, I've seen Trieste's roughest slums and the battlefields of Gelibolu. I won't be in Turkey that long and I'd hate to miss the opportunity to see the old part of Istanbul."

Nadji and Halide arrived at Galata Bridge just in time to see the late afternoon sun's reflection sparkling off the Golden Horn. Halide turned toward the Bosphorous. "Oh, look!" she exclaimed, excitedly. She pointed to a small rowboat, fifty feet offshore. A man was broiling fish over a small brazier. At Nadji's signal, he rowed toward them. Within moments, the two young people were happily munching crisp, hot mackerel fillets, covered with sliced tomato and onion, and sandwiched between thick slices of broad-grained bread. Nadji purchased two glasses of freshly-squeezed orange juice from a vendor, who carried a large brass tankard on his back. When they finished, they continued their walk up the hill and into the heart of the old city.

"Has the grand bazaar changed since the war?" she asked.

"*Kapali Charshi* is still the largest and oldest covered market in the Muslim world," he said proudly. "There are more than four thousand shops under the same roof. Even now, you can find things here that are unavailable anyplace else, but the prices are beyond my means. I haven't been here since the war ended."

It was twilight. The main streets were only dimly lit. "I think it's time we started back," Nadji said, slightly nervous. "We're close enough to Galata Bridge to make it across. It's far safer on the other side." They'd gone about a hundred yards when they heard footsteps behind them. They sped up. Whoever was behind them came closer. Neither Nadji nor Halide looked back. The lights of Pera were a quarter mile away. Suddenly, Halide was bumped and rudely shoved into a small alley adjacent to the road. Nadji was grabbed and pinioned against the wall of a building.

"Well, well, Arslanian, look what we have here," the larger of the two rough-garbed men said to his partner. "A big, Ottoman warrior and his little Turkish 'lady.' Ugly as sin and all bent-over."

"Yes, but she'll do. As my father used to say, 'In the dark, all cats are gray.'" He laughed obscenely.

Nadji struggled valiantly, but he was held fast. The first man was as tall as he, much heavier, and reeked of garlic.

"Shall I soften her up?"

"Why not? You'll get to be first."

The smaller man, about thirty, nearly Nadji's height, had a greasy mustache. As Nadji watched horrified, the man punched Halide's jaw with the heel of his palm. She started to fall backward. He reached out and cuffed her on the back of her head. Halide fell to the cobblestone ground. She started screaming at the top of her lungs. Her attacker kicked her sharply in her lower back. She moaned, involuntarily. The man opened his pants, took out his penis and urinated onto her face. "That's what I think of you Turks," he growled.

Having defiled her, his member hardened. "Up on your knees, Turkish slut," he ordered. Halide didn't move. He kicked her hard, in the ribs. "I said, *get up on your knees, do you hear me, you miserable Turkish cunt?*" he shouted.

Halide rolled over, moaning. "Get up on your knees, you whore, or I am going to put my fine Armenian prick into your mouth, right where you are." The young woman lay there, writhing in agony. Nadji tried everything to escape his tormentor's iron grip. Halide's attacker lifted her dress and rudely shove his hardened penis into her from behind. The brute plunged in and out of his rag-doll victim, mouthing obscenities.

With a strength he didn't know he possessed, Nadji broke loose from his captor and cried out in frustrated guilt and rage. Before he could get to Halide, the giant Armenian punched him in the kidney with the force of a jackhammer. Nadji collapsed, his pain so great he could hardly think.

Having ejaculated, the second Armenian rolled away from the brutally ravished young woman, his phallus exposed, going limp. A slender man emerged from the shadows. Nadji heard a soft clunk. Halide's rapist gasped, startled. The mysterious rescuer kicked the prostrate man in the groin. As Halide's torturer reached down to protect himself, the silver glint of a blade plunged into his side. Nadji's burly captor stood frozen for an instant, then took a heavy knife from his own tunic and leapt forward, arcing it in a downward motion toward the slender stranger.

A loud blast shattered the night. Nadji turned automatically toward the sound and saw a uniformed Internal Security Policeman. The heavy Armenian did not even realize his arm had been shot off, nor did he know anything else after that. The officer fired two more shots at point blank range. What had been the Armenian's head was mangled pulp. Meanwhile, the first man who'd come on the scene kicked Halide's assailant in the face, then in the stomach. With a loud whoosh of air, the fellow went limp.

"Better get your friend out of here," the officer rasped harshly to Nadji. "There's bound to be trouble."

"But you...?"

"I don't need your help. I can take care of things very well by myself."

Nadji and the slender man carried the semi-conscious Halide to a nearby fountain. The man extracted a handkerchief from his pocket, dipped it in cool water and started to bathe Halide's head. Suddenly, they heard the sound of another gunshot and the pathetic moan of a mortally-wounded animal.

Nadji extricated himself long enough to run toward the sound. The policeman had disappeared. Where Halide's attacker's genitals had been, there was a mass of blood and tissue. No matter how great his anger, Nadji prayed the man was already dead. He saw a card on the ground beside the bloody remains. With shaking hands, he picked it up and read, "*Osmanlı Kardeshlik*." Ottoman Brotherhood? But the man had been wearing a Security Police uniform. Nadji hurried back to Halide and the man who was helping her.

Halide looked up at her rescuer. Her eyes widened with recognition. "Turhan?"

"It's been a long time, Halide. We must get you to a hospital as soon as possible."

"Can you contact Doctor Ermenek?"

"I'll try. My employer lives close by. I'm sure he'll let us use his automobile to drive you there."

Nadji watched in silence, humiliated. The young man turned toward him. "Don't blame yourself. It could have happened to anyone. These are bad times. I'm Turhan Türkoğlu. Sorry I didn't have time to introduce myself before now."

Doctor Ermenek was horrified when he concluded his examination. "Halide, my dear, dear child, I can't even think of anything I could say to lessen your pain. There are no broken bones. As for the other …" The physician broke down in tears. "I can only beg you not to hold it against Turkey. What happened to you is a disgrace to our people." He dabbed at his eyes and blew into a handkerchief. "We don't even have control of our own streets anymore."

"Papa?" Halide said dully. "If Metin were alive …"

It was Yujel's wife, Françoise, who took control of the situation. "Darling, it will take time for your spirit to heal. Yujel, I think that on our way home we should stop in Switzerland. Karl Feldkirche has a friend, Doctor Jung, who might be able to help our Halide try to make some sense out of the monstrous tragedy that occurred.

A few nights later, Turhan was invited to dinner at the Akdemirs' home. "Nadji told me you were born in a small village in Anatolia," the general said to him. "How did you end up in Istanbul?"

"I moved to Diyarbakır when I was quite young. When I was fifteen, I joined a caravan and traveled to Sinop. Through good fortune, I earned enough to enable me to attend the lycée in Istanbul. When the war started, I enlisted in the medical corps. I've kept a journal since I was thirteen. Someone suggested I send some of my entries to the newspapers in Istanbul. I did, and I was quite surprised when *Vatan* published them. I enjoyed seeing my name in print. More important, I wanted to tell the world the truth as I saw it. When the war ended, there wasn't much opportunity for a writer and certainly not enough money to justify the newspapers hiring an extra reporter. They had trouble paying their existing staff. I had money saved from my caravan days. Istanbul was still the most exciting place I knew. So I stayed on. I wait tables at *Rouge et Noir*. It's honest work. When I can, I write odd pieces for a couple of small newspapers. They pay virtually nothing, but it's a start."

"You want to be a reporter?"

"No, Sir. I want to get people to think, not just blindly accept anything they read."

"That's a dangerous practice, young man. You'll make many enemies."

"I'm aware of that, Sir. One of the newspapers already got a warning letter from the Allied High Command about some of my articles."

"What are your future plans?"

"I'll send in articles and knock on doors until I eventually find full-time work with a newspaper, even if they pay me half what I make now. I believe in myself. If I work at what I love as hard as I can, perhaps Allah will do the rest."

"I have an old friend who publishes a small paper in Samsun," Akdemir said. "Would you be willing to leave the capital if I could find you employment there? It might not pay much, but at least it would be steady work."

"General, I'd work anywhere in the world if it allows me to express my thoughts," Turhan answered. At evening's end, General Akdemir suggested that Turhan spend the night in Shishli rather than chance the dangers of Stamboul.

"Omer, you devil, what are you doing in this backwater?" Ihsan Selimiye hugged his former Young Turk conspirator with genuine warmth. "It's been a dozen years since I've seen you."

"Indeed, Ihsan. The last days of Abdül Hamid. The good old days. I never could figure out why modern Turkey's most eloquent voice dropped out and moved halfway across the country."

"Safety, my friend. Much easier to write from five hundred miles away, where I could disappear onto the Anatolian steppe if they tried to chase me. Besides, why would the Ottoman government bother with a small newspaper coming out of nowhere? The decision was easy, Omer. A quiet, safe place where I could raise my children. People buy as many papers here as anywhere. Samsun's the center of the Black Sea coast. *Isharet*'s been good to me. I see you haven't done badly yourself. You still haven't told me what you're doing in town."

"I was wondering if you could use a talented young writer."

"Come now, Omer, you didn't come out of your way to find a job for your son. Besides, I heard he was following in his father's illustrious footsteps at the Military Academy."

"You don't miss much, do you?"

"Not if I can help it. *Isharet's* got friends in the capital," Ihsan chuckled. A dozen years before, he'd been the Empire's most astute reporter, capable of ferreting out any story wherever it broke. This talent had made him invaluable to the underground movement early in the century. When Ihsan had moved from Istanbul, he'd chosen his location shrewdly. Samsun was the only Black Sea city east of Zonguldak that connected directly with the Anatolian railway system, the only one with a paved road that led to the interior of the country. Although the eternal west winds, and the perennial rain did not make it the most equable place to live, the hills surrounding the town were green and provided protection from the harsh winter snows that fell farther south.

"Where can we talk in private, Ihsan?"

"*Isharet's* back office. Do I sense something afoot?"

"When we get to your place we'll talk." They reached the newspaper plant fifteen minutes later. The day's only edition had already been distributed. The place was closed. Ihsan unlocked the front door, walked through a large room that housed printing presses, and led his guest to a small office deep within the building. The furniture in the room was old, but serviceable. The two friends sat opposite one another in cracked leather chairs.

"Now you have your privacy, Omer. Were you serious when you asked if I needed another reporter?"

"I was. A month ago, Nadji brought home a young man who calls himself 'Turhan Türkoğlu.'"

"Two names, no less. And 'Son of Turkey' at that. Rather pretentious, wouldn't you say?"

"I seem to recall a young man who called himself 'The Voice of the new Turkey.' Rather pretentious, wouldn't you say?"

"Touché!"

"Turhan came out of nowhere and saved Nadji's and his friend Halide's life. I'll tell you that story another time. I've talked with him at length. Reminds me a lot of you. Take that as a compliment."

The publisher stroked his chin, thoughtfully. "Have you seen any of his work?"

"Yes. He's written a few pieces for *Mimber*."

The publisher glanced over the articles Akdemir had brought with him. "Not bad. Strident, but they show promise. Do you want me to hire the boy?"

"No pressure from me one way or the other. With or without you, he'll have a successful career. You just might speed it up a bit."

"Oho! 'No pressure from you,' and you immediately tell me the fellow will have a fine career. Omer, I've seen too many journalists with great careers ahead of them. Twenty years later, those careers are still ahead of them. They lose themselves in the *rakı* bars, or they move on to other things. It's a tough life. It has a way of eating a man's soul."

"What do you have to lose, Ihsan? You're in Samsun. You can get away with paying someone half what he'd cost you in Istanbul. If he's good, you can say you gave him his start."

"All right, you've twisted my arm hard enough. I'll try him and see how he works out."

"You'll be thanking me within six months."

"Enough. You didn't haul me into the confines of my private office to ask me to hire a novice reporter. What's your news?"

"A story that'll put *Isharet* in Turkish history books."

"Go on."

"Mustafa Kemal's coming here."

"That's not news. Damad appointed him inspector general of the Ninth Army. He's on his way to Samsun on the *Bandırma*, a cargo ship the government bought from the Greeks."

The general reached into his tunic and brought out a barely legible, crumpled carbon of a typewritten document. "Read this."

"*'To All Military and Civilian Authorities, From His Imperial Eminence and Grace Vahideddin, Sultan Mehmet VI:*

'Please take notice that the Sultan's own representative, Mustafa Kemal Pasha, is herewith afforded the mandate of this office to gather all arms and ammunition and restore order and security to His Majesty's ports, cities and towns throughout Anatolia and those areas referred to by the Allied High Command as the Pontic States. Whoever reads this proclamation and the seal thereon is directed, in Our name, to afford Mustafa Kemal Pasha all courtesy and governance, with the full authority of the Ottoman Empire over all military and civilian officials in the Anatolian provinces...'"

Ihsan stopped reading. His face colored. "Mashallah! Do you know how much power that gives him?"

"I do. So does Kemal."

"Why the conspiratorial grin?"

"Ihsan, how many newspapers can you print from this moment forward if your presses run day and night?"

"Thirty thousand copies in each twenty-four hour period, assuming we've got enough newsprint in storage."

"Can you buy newsprint from your competitors?"

"Without them becoming suspicious? Hardly. Why?"

"Two days ago, twenty thousand Greek troops landed at Izmir. As we speak, they're advancing toward Manisa and Aydin, with British and French protection. They've inflicted severe atrocities on the Turkish civilian population. A Turkish colonel, who refused to take off his fez and stamp on it, was shot and killed. The Turkish governor of Izmir was arrested. Hundreds of civilians on both sides have been killed. The Greeks believe they've opened the gateway to the conquest of Anatolia."

"I learned that by telephone. How did our government in Istanbul react?"

"'Heroically,'" the general said, sarcastically. "Mehmet started blubbering in public. His ministers filed a 'protest' with the Allied High Command. The 'government,' such as it is, seems prepared to sacrifice all of Turkey so long as Istanbul remains Ottoman."

The editor sighed. "Omer, what did we Young Turks really accomplish?" he asked, rhetorically. "We knocked Abdül Hamid, the last strong sultan, off the throne a decade ago. What did it gain us? A weak puppet who dares call himself sultan, three proud pashas who led us into a disastrous war, and now the triumphant western Allies carving us up like a dead lamb. Where's it all going to lead?"

"Listen, Ihsan. An unusually large number of soldiers and officers will be coming east in the next few days. Four days from now, May 19, Kemal will anchor off Samsun. As soon as he steps ashore, he'll announce his intent to form an independent Turkish republic."

"*WHAT???* You know that means civil war."

"Within the next month, Kemal intends to set up armed resistance to the Greek incursion."

"You're certain, Omer?"

"Absolutely."

"You know what it will do to my reputation, not to mention my pocketbook, if you're wrong?"

"I'm not wrong, Ihsan. Have I lied to you in the past?"

"Never."

"Start your presses now. Use only people you can trust to keep quiet about this until Mustafa Kemal gets here. Buy up as much paper and ink as you can. Detail someone to be as close as a shadow to Kemal for the next year."

"You've no doubt someone in mind for the job?"

"Does 'The Voice of the New Turkey' want to become a reporter once again?"

"Hardly, my friend. I'm too old and too fat. You have confidence in this young fellow, Turhan?"

"That's entirely up to you."

"So it will cost me a few lira. If you're right, I can certainly spare that. Where's my newest employee?"

"On his way to Samsun. He'll be here on the next train."

On May 19, 1919, the winds raised the Black Sea outside Samsun harbor to a rough chop. Small boats came out from the beach to meet the grimy cargo ship and row the new inspector general and his staff ashore. Mustafa Kemal landed at a rickety wooden jetty, and slogged ashore through shallow water. He was greeted by four officers, one of whom was Omer Akdemir. They took the *Pasha* to an old house off the main square, where he set up headquarters. A few hundred yards down the dusty street, three Allied officers were busily shuffling papers. They'd not even bothered to take the time to meet the new arrival.

4

June 10, 1920   *Ankara*
Mlle. Halide Orhan
Associate Professor of Education
18-B, Rue Besançon
Paris, France

Dear Halide:

Has it really been six months since I've written you? So incredibly much has happened since the beginning of the year I don't know how or where to begin. I'm writing from Angora, which the nationalist government has renamed Ankara. *You don't know how happy it makes Turhan and me to hear you'll be coming here within the next couple of months.*

Last year, father talked Ihsan into hiring Turhan. From the day they met, each served as a catalyst for the other. Ihsan, who hadn't put pen to paper in years, took to writing again. Between them Isharet's *circulation trebled. Mustafa Kemal gave Turhan an exclusive interview. When he said he relied on* Isharet *for "accurate and patriotic reporting," the number of readers soared. Last month Isharet opened its Ankara bureau. Turhan was named chief, at the ripe old age of twenty-three.*

Congratulations on your graduation from the Sorbonne and your certification as associate professor of education. I'm gratified you want to teach in Turkey. We need all the help we can get!

You're probably curious how I got here. After Kemal's nationalists won elections throughout Anatolia, they demanded their seats in the Ottoman Chamber of Deputies. Kemal announced his party was Turkey's rightful government. At that point, all hell broke loose. The British pushed the Sultan into declaring martial law in Istanbul. Allied troops replaced Ottoman police, the Chamber was dissolved, and Damad Ferid – remember "Droopy Damad?" – was called back to suppress the outbreaks.

Father aligned himself with Kemal's new government in Ankara. Within a month, I was asked to leave the Academy. The commandant was embarrassed. He'd received orders from general staff. He said with Father working for Kemal in Ankara, I'd have divided loyalties. It was very smoothly done, but it hurt a lot to be dumped out in my senior year.

Father was furious and tried to talk to his old friends at the Academy, but to no avail. For the next month, I sulked in Shishli, until Father told us we were moving to Ankara. He explained that Ankara's Grand National Assembly had ordered the creation of a new, nationalist officers' school. He'd been appointed its first commandant! If the new government works out, I'll be able to say I was in the first graduating class of the Turkish Military Academy of Ankara. I wasn't really surprised at Father's announcement because I'd been in touch with Turhan, who somehow managed to get a telephone hookup between Ankara and Istanbul. He kept me well posted.

You'll find things unsettled when you get here. There's a civil war going on between Istanbul and Ankara. So far, it's only a war of words, but it's had ludicrous side effects. A tribunal from Istanbul condemned Kemal to death. The Sheikh of Islam made it the religious duty of any Muslim to kill him on sight. The Grand National Assembly retaliated by convicting Damad Ferid and sentencing him to death. Several local Muslim leaders decreed it was the duty of their congregants to kill Ferid.

What makes this all the more idiotic is regardless of which government we support, Turkey is fighting a two front war, Armenians in the east, Greeks in the west. To top everything off, a group of irregulars calling themselves the "Green Army" – nobody really knows whose side they're on – announced that they're going to war against the Christian invaders.

If this all sounds confusing to you, it's even more of a mix-up living in the middle of it. Let me know when you plan to arrive so Turhan and I can be there to meet you.

In fondest friendship, Nadji

Ankara was less than impressive. Twin hills rose from the sere Anatolian plateau. The half-ruined walls of a citadel, which had survived two thousand years of wars, sat atop one of the hills. Mud-brick shacks, huddled together amid dunghills and dirt alleyways, descended into the dusty valley below. Raw sewage ran down the middle of these "streets." The odor of frying onions and garlic dominated Ulus' "Golden Hill." Horses drew ramshackle carriages over rough stones. Except for a very few motor cars, the only means of transport were ancient buckboards and bullock carts. The nationalist mecca was hardly more than a small market town. Its population had been reduced to twenty thousand by a fire that had wiped out a large segment of the place during the past war. Blackened remains of buildings still scarred the slopes. A low ridge of brown, inhospitable hills surrounded the southern end of town.

Still, as she alighted from the station platform, Halide saw that Ankara was starting to grow into a city. The administration had erected new public buildings in the spare, modern European style. Houses were starting to dot the plain beyond Citadel hill. The city boasted a small municipal park, unkempt, ragged, its flowers and grass drying up in the brutal sun. But it was a beginning.

Halide linked arms with her two comrades and gaily said, "Well, here we are, three heroes of modern Turkey, reunited once again. What will we do to change the course of history this time?"

"Locate a good juice vendor?" suggested Nadji.

"Better yet, find some kind of decent lodgings in this town," remarked Turhan.

"Come now, you boys can do better than that for a Parisian lady who's come so many miles just to be with you."

"I wish we could," Nadji replied. "The best accommodations we can provide are at my family's house on Chankaya hill, outside the city proper."

"Take advantage of it," said Turhan. "At least there you'll be above all the dust and smoke of the valley."

As they descended to the street, Halide's eyes widened in pleasure. "Isn't that the old Mercedes?"

"The very one you rode in when you first came to Turkey! Amazing how time flies, isn't it."

"The car looks so well-kept. And quite out of place in Ankara."

"It's both," Nadji responded, laughing. "Father's commandeered one of only six of these behemoths in the capital. It's his one luxury, though a rather impractical one. With the streets in such abominable condition, he has to order new tires every couple of months."

The three friends stopped for tea in Yenishehir, Ankara's "new city," and caught up on a year's worth of news. "Will there ever be anything but fighting and more fighting in Turkey?" Halide asked, seriously.

"*Inshallah*, some day there'll be peace. Progress as well, we hope," answered Turhan. "I started out life in a village in southeastern Anatolia. Now I'm an 'up and coming' journalist. Less than one person out of every ten in Turkey can read what I write. We must educate our countrymen so we can communicate with one another on the most basic level. It's a miracle we can mount any army at all."

"Perhaps one day we'll really be able to do something for our country."

"Yes, but we'll need a few years of peace to do it. Unfortunately, it doesn't appear we'll have that opportunity in the foreseeable future. The Greek offensive, which started three weeks ago, has turned into a rout. Just yesterday, they captured Gelibolu."

In October, 1920, young King Alexander of Greece was watching the antics of a pair of monkeys in his palace gardens, when he was bitten by one of them and died. The English statesman Winston Churchill wrote, "It is no exaggeration to remark that a quarter million persons died because of the monkey's bite."

After Alexander's death, Premier Venizelos declared a general election. He was so certain of his popularity that he gave his countrymen full freedom to cast their ballots any way they wanted. They promptly voted him out of office. King Constantine, who'd been discredited and exiled in 1917 for complicity with the Germans, was restored to the throne. The Greeks determined to push forward all the way to Armenia and create the greatest empire since Alexander the Great.

They planned to move east along the railway, unite all their forces in Anatolia and cut the Turks' communications. By the end of winter, they'd be poised to smash Ankara and Konya, twin Muslim rallying points. On January 6, 1921, they attacked along a broad front, stretching from Eskishehir to Bursa. The first clash took place in the valley of Inönü.

The Greeks expected an easy victory against undisciplined, ill-equipped, and demoralized peasants and irregulars. Instead, they found themselves facing a resolute, disciplined force under Ismet Pasha, Mustafa Kemal's deputy and second in command. The Turks were greatly inferior in numbers and equipment, but not in leadership and fighting spirit. Knee deep in mud and snow, they stubbornly defended their own territory. Four days later, Constantine's previously invincible forces retreated, stunned, to Bursa. The Greeks would have to contend with a new kind of Turkish army.

On March 23, the Greeks began a new offensive. Afyon fell to the Royal Hellenic army, but General Ismet's forces prevailed at Inönü, and Ismet later took on Inönü as his surname. The Greek forces retreated again. Ernest Hemingway, a young American correspondent with the Greeks, wrote, "Constantine's newly arrived officers didn't know a god-damned thing about how to run a war. Their artillery fired into their own troops. It was the first time I'd seen dead men wearing white ballet skirts and upturned shoes with pompons on them. The Turks just kept coming, steadily and lumpily, without show, without glamour. But they kept coming."

In early June, Constantine proclaimed himself supreme commander of Greek forces in Asia, and left for Smyrna. He vowed to be the first Christian king to set foot on Anatolian soil in a thousand years. He did not enter the port, but stayed across the gulf at Cheshme on the western tip of Anatolia, the same place from which Richard *Coeur de Lion* commenced the first Crusade. By the third week in July, the Greeks had advanced to the Sakarya River, the last natural boundary before the nationalist capital. In Ankara, the Grand National Assembly prepared to move east, all the way to Sivas.

"Congratulations, Lieutenant! Since I'm the first to salute you, military tradition requires you pay me one Turkish lira. And I certainly don't intend to give credit to a soldier."

Nadji returned the salute, took the oldest, most rumpled **Ottoman** bill he could find from his wallet, and pressed it into the outstretched hand.

"Cheap Nationalist!" Turhan replied, grinning. "That won't even buy a man a glass of *rakı*. I'll show you how gracious I am by allowing you to buy me a cup of tea and a piece of baklava." The two young men soon reached their favorite haunt.

"Have you seen Halide lately?" Nadji asked.

"No," Turhan replied. "She asked Kemal to be assigned to duty at the front. Dropped her teacher's garb for a nurse's uniform. Do you have any idea where you'll be assigned?"

"I'll tell you after we've left."

As they departed the tea house, Turhan asked, "Why the secrecy, Nadji?"

"The information's sensitive. The less said, the better."

"Understood, my friend. What's the news?"

"Two weeks ago, the Greeks captured Eskishehir. Ismet retreated to the Sakarya."

"That's nothing the world doesn't know."

"Less than three hours ago, Mustafa Kemal agreed to become commander-in-chief on condition he be authorized to exercise all powers normally given to the Grand National Assembly, for the next three months."

"That's political suicide!"

"That Grand National Assembly agreed to it."

"*Mashallah!!*"

"*Mashallah's* right! He's going to proclaim that every household in Ankara'll be required to provide a pair of underclothing, socks and sandals to the war effort. The army's requisitioning all men's clothing in every store in Ankara. They've appropriated forty percent of all food and gasoline supplies. Kemal says the government will pay for these things later. Every vehicle owner must provide free transportation for the army."

"He won't be too popular here."

"There's more," Nadji continued. "He's ordered one out of every five farm animals and carts in the city to be given up. Anyone with a rifle, gun, or ammunition must surrender it to the army. Everything – *everything* – is being shipped to the front at the Sakarya. But I still haven't told you the big news."

"There's more?"

"Kemal himself is going to command the Sakarya front."

"WHAT???"

"Kemal says if he's going to take full responsibility he wants full authority as well."

"That could be the story of the century as far as Turkey's concerned!"

"Kemal's staked Turkey's whole future on victory at the Sakarya. He's sending every available officer, soldier, and reserve unit to the front. Father will be commanding a division. I'm being sent to an artillery unit. If the Greeks win this battle, there's nothing between the river and the capital. The war will be over."

"Can I get there to cover the story??"

"Talk to Kemal's chief of staff. Use your influence. You're well-liked. The story'll be bigger than Gallipoli."

"*Inshallah!* Let us only pray it ends as well for us."

5

Nadji arrived at Polatlı. He was self-conscious when he reported to his commander in a new, fitted uniform. The short, stocky captain was dressed in battle fatigues that looked as if he'd worn them, unchanged, for ten years.

"Lieutenant Akdemir reporting for duty, Sir!" Nadji snapped his best Academy salute.

"At ease, Lieutenant," the commander, whose name was Merich, said. "You from the Academy?"

"Yes, Sir."

"Ever seen battle?"

Before he could answer, a grubby-looking lieutenant, with three days' growth of whiskers, rudely interrupted. "Are you kidding? Look at him. Academy spit-and-polish. They all fall apart in the field. I can't understand why they send us the useless ones. Might as well stay home with their mamas."

"That's quite enough, Erdal," the captain said.

"Oh is it? These precious Academy types get the best quarters, the best food, the best assignments. They throw us into the field as expendable."

"We're all in this together, Lieutenant," Nadji said coldly. "Once upon a time you went into your first battle. No doubt you're the bravest hero that ever lived. But I'm here to do my part. I don't need permission from you. Understand?"

Captain Merich watched the exchange in silence. He addressed Nadji. "Akdemir, you'll learn quickly enough. If that uniform's as stiff and uncomfortable as it looks, you should report to the quartermaster and get outfitted. You get one set of clothes for the duration."

"How long'll that be, Captain?" He felt stupid the moment the words escaped his lips. Erdal sneered.

The captain looked at Nadji. "The Greeks say they'll fight 'til they get to Ankara. Only fifty miles between here and there."

"How many men in our regiment, Sir?"

"Two hundred on paper. A third of 'em have been killed in the last few days. We're supposed to get ten thousand reinforcements. You're the first they've sent this week. Is your father by any chance General Akdemir?" the captain asked.

"Yes, Sir. But I'm not asking any favors on his account."

"You won't get any. Mustafa Kemal's stripped *himself* of all rank. You'll be in charge of 'D' company."

"I've never held a command, Sir."

"Don't worry, Lieutenant. Just about every commanding officer left can say much the same thing."

"What am I supposed to do, Sir?"

"Kill. And avoid being killed."

Nadji awoke to the scratching of a small ground animal. It was still dark. His back ached from sleeping in a sitting position in the trench. He wrapped himself tighter in the woolen blanket, grateful he could still feel hot and cold. It seemed like ten years rather than ten days since he'd arrived at the front. Nothing had prepared him for the grim reality of battle. Generals and politicians could talk all they wanted about the glory of the motherland and the valor of heroic warriors. When it got down to bedrock, war was an ugly, terrifying business, filled with the smell of gunpowder, feces, vomit, and blood. Merich had been a good man. Erdal had been a bastard. Now they were both dead, cut down by rifle fire three days ago, defending a hill so low it didn't have a name.

Dawn brightened the sky in the east. Praise Allah the ground was more solid underneath him. Yesterday had been the worst. Normally the broiling summer sun of the Anatolian steppe turned the soil to rock as it beat down without mercy. By sunset last evening, corpses littered every yard of ground. The earth had become mushy, unable to soak up the blood spilled earlier in the day. The survivors had to be careful where they walked. Supper had been grim. Last night, much of the day's bread was soaked with his comrades' blood. Those who were still alive tore off dry pieces wherever they could find them. That was all there was. Water was in such short supply that after dark the survivors stumbled over dead bodies, searching for canteens.

When Nadji assumed command of "D" company, thirty-two of the original forty men were alive: tough, battle-hardened veterans, particularly the company sergeant, all of twenty-two years old. By the time battle had ceased the night before, ten of his company would never rise again.

He heard the rustle of animals scurrying about. "Rats!" The sergeant whispered the words harshly. "Ignore 'em, Sir."

But they were hard to disregard. Several rodents crawled over the face of the nearest corpse, sniffing, squealing, tearing what skin and flesh remained. Nadji raised his rifle. "Don't, Sir!" the sergeant whispered in the same tone. "It'll alert the enemy. All you'll do is waste what little ammunition we've got left."

"Did the troops find anything we can use?"

"A few rounds, Lieutenant. For the most part, the shells were spent."

"Any idea how many troops are on this hill?"

"Eighty living. Maybe. Five hundred dead."

"What do we do with the bodies, Sergeant?"

"Nothing you *can* do, Sir. Let 'em rot and hope Allah takes them before the vultures do. It'll be worse today than yesterday. The flies'll gather in droves."

Their conversation stopped. They sensed another man crawling toward them. "Who's in charge here?" the voice asked.

"Lieutenant Akdemir, 'D' company. Who're you?"

"Karaja, Seventeenth Regiment. What's your troop strength, Lieutenant?"

"Twenty-two last count." He saw captain's insignia on the newcomer. "Yours?"

"Twenty."

"Which company, Captain?"

"The *regiment*."

"Allah! How many did you lose yesterday?"

"A hundred fifty."

Within two hours of daylight, the flies started their horrendous buzz. They picked at the faces of dead soldiers strewn over the hillside. The sun beat down on the sweating men. There was no fresh water anywhere. Despite a stray shot here and there, the silence of the vast steppe was overwhelming. Nadji saw dark smudge lines on the distant horizon. The enemy. He heard the crack of gunfire. It was so distant it didn't disturb nearby ground squirrels.

Some soldiers took naps. Others gambled, trying to guess how many small stones were under a helmet placed on the ground. When the sun reached its zenith, Nadji heard a soft moan and turned to his right. A boy of seventeen keeled over, a victim of heat prostration. Nadji grabbed the fellow's canteen to pour out some water. It was empty. He unscrewed the cap on his own container. Nothing.

"Anyone got water?" he asked quietly.

No one had.

"We can't go on like this," the sergeant said. "Another day without water, we'll all be like him."

"What do we do about him, Sergeant?"

"Nothing. Let him die, Sir."

"You can't mean that!"

"Just what do you expect me to do?" the sergeant asked. "Do you have any ideas about how we get water? I suppose we could cut into one of the corpses and see if there's any blood left."

The young man's moans became more pronounced. A man crawled toward them on his belly, leaving a trail of blood behind him. When he'd gotten to their hole, Nadji saw the man's shoes were soaked in blood. His eyes were rolling up into his head.

"L... Lieutenant..." he wheezed. "I'm dying. Take my water." He belched up warm blood, rolled into the trench alongside them, and was silent. Nadji uttered a prayer over the dead man. He tore a piece of material off the dead man's uniform and poured a few drops of water on the cloth. He applied the patch to the dehydrated boy's lips. When the fellow finally regained consciousness, he was weak and his eyes were fluttery.

"Captain, we've got to get word to command for reinforcements, food, water."

"I agree, Lieutenant. Any idea where we might locate battalion command?"

"Back of the line somewhere."

"Where do you think the 'line' is?"

"I don't know. We can't stay here without help. By day after tomorrow, we'll be nothing but food for the rats." Some time during the previous day, he couldn't say when, his terror and fear had disappeared. He was a very small piece of a fighting machine. If he did his job and the small cogs in the wheel next to him did *their* jobs, the machine would operate. Now he had to find fuel for the human element of that machine, and keep his little piece of earth Turkish. Nothing else mattered. "Do you have a map, Captain?"

"An old one."

"It'll do."

The two men spent the next hour poring over a detailed, crumpled chart of the area. "We'll have to guess the best we can," Nadji said. "We're most likely on this rise," he said, pointing. The highest point, *Chal Dağ*, is four miles east. As far as I can tell, we're the only Turkish officers between here and there. One of us has to stay put. I think it'd be best if it were you, Sir. You're senior and have more experience. We'll have to gamble I can get through. If I'm not back by tomorrow night, you'll know I didn't make it."

"*Allah's marladik*, Lieutenant," the other officer said. "Go with God."

The sun set. Nadji headed down and around the rise, moving slowly, from bush to bush. The countryside to the east was low. It did not appear to have seen much fighting. He saw lights on a hill to the east. *Inshallah, let them be Turkish*, he prayed silently.

He was halfway across the valley when he heard a shuffling sound. More rats? He didn't know. The sound became louder. As he turned, Nadji saw a man running toward him. The stranger's rifle was raised, the bayonet aimed at him.

His first thought was, "Allah, don't let me die!" The next was, "Don't let him be a Turk!" He spun round, dove for the ground, and dodged as the other man swiped at him. He ripped a dagger from his belt and struck at the back of the man's leg. With a shocked scream, his assailant went down. No time to think. Nadji struck again and again, plunging his dagger into soft flesh wherever he could find it. The man's body convulsed, then collapsed in a heap.

When Nadji finally recovered enough to stop stabbing, his hand was wet and sticky. The other man gurgled. Nadji's eyes became accustomed to the dark. His attacker wouldn't be getting up again. Bile churned in his throat. He lurched a few yards from the dying man and retched until he felt his insides would come out. He still didn't know if his assailant was Greek or Turk. Was he alone? If he wasn't, Nadji knew that anyone within fifty yards would have heard the scuffle. He found a shallow burrow, twenty feet from where the man lay, and waited.

Twenty minutes went by. The man continued to emit a bubbling noise as he strained to breathe. Nadji tried to cover his ears to blot out the horrible sound. When he did, he noticed his own head was wet. Putting his fingers to his lips, he tasted blood. Odd, he didn't feel particularly weak. Instinctively, he gathered dirt and rubbed it against his head. Probably just grazed by the bayonet. Then realization hit. An inch either way and he would be the one gurgling in his death throes, not the other man.

An hour passed. The bubbling sound had become a dry rasp. The man was dying. Nadji crawled over, possessed by morbid curiosity. The other – he was wearing a Greek uniform, praise Allah – opened his eyes and stared at him with a look of utter terror. His body lay still, silent. His eyes confronted Nadji with an expression the young lieutenant would never forget. Resignation? Accusation? Anger?

The dying man worked his mouth half open and tried to speak. No sound came. Nadji stared back at him. The overwhelming magnitude of what he'd done struck home. This was not a nameless, faceless enemy. Not like shooting across a vast field, tossing a grenade into an enemy concentration. Not even the same as seeing his comrades fall. He was witnessing the death of another human being, a death he had caused. Nadji moved closer. With superhuman effort, the man tried to say something. Nothing came out.

Nadji reached for his canteen and opened it. Only a few drops of water left. They'd be wasted on a dead man. He looked at the other man's face again. The look was helpless, condemning. Nadji poured the last few drops onto the sleeve of his tunic. He pressed the moistened sleeve against the dying man's mouth. The eyes ceased their anger and became softer.

"May your God bless you," Nadji said softly. Were the man's eyes actually forgiving? Nadji never knew. A moment later they were sightless. The man was dead.

Nadji felt a chill. His face was wet, but now the wetness was from tears, not blood. An hour ago, a moment ago, this man had lived, breathed, spoken with his comrades. Praise Allah, he'd killed a Greek. At least it was the enemy. Did he have a wife? A mother? Was the Greek any less of a man because he was fighting under a different set of generals? For different politicians?

Nadji rolled the corpse over and saw a wallet in the man's back pocket. He removed it with trembling hands. Two pictures and a letter fell out. A quarter-moon had risen in the night sky. Nadji hadn't even noticed it before. No wonder it had been so easy to see the man's eyes. He couldn't read the strange lettering on the envelope. There were two photographs. A small, dark-haired woman with a serious face, stood alone in the first one. In the second, she was flanked on each side by a little girl, each with braided hair. The man's daughters? The thought pierced Nadji like a dagger thrust into his chest.

There was an identity card written in Greek and in English, which Nadji had learned to read at the Academy. It identified the dead man as Nikos Stamoulatos, twenty-three, school teacher. Nadji did not make it back to the hole in time. He wept openly and vomited what little remained inside of him.

Shortly before noon next day, Nadji made it to the distant hill where he found a large Turkish force. Nadji told the division commander, a full colonel, what had happened. Just before he collapsed from fatigue, he heard the senior officer order a thousand reinforcements be sent immediately to bring food and water to their compatriots who suffered, half-dead, on the small rise with no name.

At sunset, a messenger came riding back to battalion headquarters. "What news?" the colonel asked.

"The valley was swarming with Greeks, Sir. We lost half our troops before we got there. The other five hundred fought their way through. We killed fifteen hundred enemy, Sir."

By the following evening, the valley was as blood-soaked as the rise had been three days before. Five hundred men retreated from whence they'd come. And five thousand didn't move at all.

On September 15, 1921, the following article occupied the entire front page of *Isharet*.

TURKEY IS SAVED! GREEKS RETREAT FROM THE SAKARYA!

Polatlı, Turkey. The battle of the Sakarya is over. No more will Ankarans go to bed each night to the fearsome sound of artillery pounding in the distance. The trains standing ready to move the government to Sivas have been unpacked. The city's lights have been turned back on. Cars brave the streets again.

A month ago, the Greek advance from the west began. For ten days, Greek troops moved forward across the steppe, ever farther from the valleys of the Aegean coast. The drought and the sun's heat were more merciless than the blizzards and frosts of earlier battles. Constantine's army carried no water tanks. His troops suffered from thirst. Their modern truck transport broke down on the rough tracks of the Turkish heartland. They had to depend, as did we, on oxcarts, camels, and pack animals. A Greek captain, who preferred not to be identified, told me his starving troops had begged bread from their Turkish captors. The dust choked them. Malaria thinned their ranks. Nevertheless, when they got to the Sakarya, Greek troops outnumbered Turks by a margin of three to two.

Mustafa Kemal set up headquarters at Polatlı railway station. Later, he moved to a half-built mud-walled house on Alagöz hill. He wore his uniform without badge or rank. He'd been dismissed from the Ottoman army and the Grand National Assembly had given him no official military status. Yet, from the very first, there was no doubt he commanded every square meter of the battlefield.

Halide Orhan, a young Turkish woman who'd been born in France, set up the field hospital behind the lines. Her compassion and coolness under fire was an inspiration and a blessing to our gallant troops.

When the fighting came, it lasted twenty-two days and nights without respite. Mustafa Kemal saw he might have to die with the rest if disaster took place. The most vicious fight was for Chal Dağ, the hill that commanded the plain all the way to Ankara. Back in the capital, I heard the cynical comment, "There are other hills between Chal Dağ and the city. If we leave five hundred Greeks dead on the summit of each, there won't be more than fifty left when they arrive here. We'll simply beat them to death with sticks." But there was no such talk at the front. The army knew the battle for Chal Dağ would decide Turkey's fate.

At Haymana, just west of Chal Dağ, the last city before Ankara, Turkish forces resisted with losses of a thousand men a day. In one instance, General Akdemir's son, a newly commissioned lieutenant, found himself in command of what was left of a battalion. An entire artillery division had only seventeen rounds left when the battle ceased.

Finally, the two armies fought to a standstill. Each was ready to retreat. But the Turkish line had held. The Greeks, too exhausted to follow up their attack on Haymana, had run out of food and water. At two o'clock in the morning, September 12, they began to retreat. By day's end, no Greek soldier remained east of the Sakarya.

Our countrymen have fought in Gelibolu and the Caucasus, in Palestine and at the gates of Istanbul. But in all the years of this century, I believe that at the Battle of the Sakarya the stolid, simple Turkish soldier, outmanned, outmaneuvered, with obsolete artillery, with horses reduced to skin and bone, achieved the greatest glory of all. The motherland was saved.

by Turhan Türkoğlu

"What do you think of our illustrious journalist, Halide?" Nadji asked over tea that evening. "I understand several newspapers outside Turkey have picked up Turhan's stories."

"Do you think that strutting dandy will ever talk to us 'lowly folk' again? Did you see him preen when the officers asked him to autograph their copies of *Isharet*?"

"If I know Turhan, that'll last a day. He's probably busy concocting a story that'll infuriate the same 'leaders' who are so anxious to get his signature today."

"I know," Halide sighed. "He's like a little boy in so many ways. He still lectures me that 'truth is an absolute thing, never a relative one.' He'll get himself in trouble one of these days."

"And you and I both know we'll be there to help him when he does. Where do you go from here, Halide?"

"I'll stay near the front. The war's not even close to being over. Turhan's words notwithstanding, when the bodies are buried, there'll be another battle and after that another."

"You sound cynical."

"No, my friend. Just a very tired woman who's already seen more battles than I ever wanted to see in my lifetime. One day we'll need to fight a different kind of war."

"What do you mean?"

"Nadji, the ordinary Turk can't read maps, he can't read orders. *He can't read.* Our people have given their brains no more exercise than trees in a forest. We need to educate our masses, give every man, woman and child a fighting chance to survive in the twentieth century. That's the battle we must fight. Unless we win *that* war, Turkey will remain a land of illiterate peasants, falling further and further behind the world every year. What will you do now?"

"I look forward to boredom. My commanding officer requested that I lead a survey party behind the mine sweepers, so we can update the army's battle charts. He said I deserved a few days of safe relaxation."

One week after the battle, Nadji, Sergeant Hüsseyin and Corporal Firat packed up their survey gear. The last measurements of the day had been made. Autumn had come to the land and a beautiful sunset lit the evening sky. "What do you say, fellows? Do we go all the way back to headquarters tonight or do we camp here?" Nadji asked his companions.

"Let's stay out here," the young corporal replied. "We've only got one more day of work. It's a long trek back to headquarters. We'd only have to come back here tomorrow morning."

"I disagree, Lieutenant," the sergeant said. "Our orders were clear. We were given our coordinates this morning and we've reached them. I say we return."

"We're already beyond the original boundaries we were given to survey," Nadji said. "We're twenty miles beyond the battle zone. I agree we shouldn't take unnecessary chances, but there can't be any harm in camping here and waiting for the mine sweepers to come through. Tell you what. We'll backtrack to that small rise and pitch our tents there overnight. Since the sweepers have covered the area already, it's bound to be safe."

The decision made, the three men chatted happily on their way to their campsite.

When the land mine exploded under their feet, Nadji saw a brilliant flash before everything went dark. The others didn't even know there was a flash. Parts of their bodies were later found over a radius of more than a hundred feet.

"General Izzet? Mustafa Kemal here." It had been remarkably easy to make telephone connections with Istanbul.

"*Gazi* Mustafa Kemal?" Izzet replied, using the honorary title "Conqueror of the Infidels," which the grateful Assembly had conferred on the commander-in-chief a few days before. "Why would my old comrade-in-arms and present 'sworn enemy' grace the 'declining' Ottoman Empire with a personal call?"

"Izzet, this has nothing to do with politics. This call never took place, understand?"

"Of course, Mustafa. What's up, my friend?"

"Omer Akdemir's boy, Nadji, was very seriously injured by a land mine explosion during the Sakarya mop-up. His leg was shattered, temporary blindness, bad burns. Naturally, we've got the best hospitals right here in Ankara, and all that political garbage, but..."

"I'll make sure there's a vehicle ready to take him to University Hospital immediately, Kemal. Doctor Ermenek will supervise the surgery. How'll you get the boy here?"

"We'll send a special hospital train. Can you arrange to help once we get to Haydarpasha?"

"Certainly."

"Thanks, Izzet. You really are a friend."

"Likewise, Mustafa. Oh, and Kemal Bey?"

"Yes?"

"You really do deserve the title *Gazi-Mushir*. Even if you've sworn to bring Sultan Vahideddin's throne toppling down. You're sure you won't reconsider?

"Too late, my friend. The die's been cast. Many, many thanks, though."

"*Allah'smahrladik!*"

"Go with God, yourself, Izzet. *Güle güle.*"

Since the Greeks occupied Eskishehir, the trains between Istanbul and Ankara, which had run on a daily basis since the completion of the line in 1892, now operated only irregularly. Neither the sultan's government in Istanbul nor the nationalists in Ankara communicated much with the other these days, so the loss was inconvenient but not critical.

Notwithstanding the raging war in Anatolia, both Turks and Greeks respected crossing of battle lines for humanitarian reasons. Thus it was that the small, wood-burning locomotive and its single hospital car left the nationalist capital on the steppe, and headed west, toward the crumbling city of the sultans.

Inside the car, Nadji was strapped to a narrow, flat cot to minimize movement. His face, where it hadn't been burned, was deathly pale. What skin was not covered by dressings and bandages was translucent. For the greatest part of the journey, he was mercifully unconscious. Only an occasional moan revealed he was still alive.

The trip from Ankara to Haydarpasha station, on the Asiatic side of the Bosphorous, took fifteen hours. Turhan and Halide accompanied their friend. They slept fitfully through the first part of the journey, which traversed dry, brown steppe, awakening when Greek authorities stopped the train at Eskishehir for a thorough inspection. Even in the midst of war, large pallets, stenciled with foreign destinations, were stacked on the platform, awaiting the next Istanbul-bound train, whenever it would arrive.

"Meerschaum," Turhan answered Halide's questioning glance. "The world's supply is mined in Eskishehir. Nowadays, most of it is shipped to Germany, where artisans have developed the carving of intricate pipes into their own art form."

West of Eskishehir, the land became progressively greener, more lush, as they approached the Sea of Marmara. Turhan and Halide felt a thrill of nervous excitement as they approached the outskirts of Asiatic Istanbul. Despite Mustafa Kemal's dream of creating a metropolis on the steppe, the decaying Ottoman capital was still *the* city.

Two hours after they passed Izmit, at the head of the Sea of Marmara, the engine pulled into Istanbul's Haydarpasha station, the ornate, gilded terminus of the Anatolian railroad, which still maintained its nineteenth century rococo elegance. They were cleared for immediate transfer by ferry to the European side of the city. Shortly after noon, Nadji was in the operating theater.

The operation on Nadji's shattered leg lasted ten hours. The burn specialists concluded there'd be no need for skin transplants. The medical team would depend on zinc compounds, constant moisturizing coolants, time, and nature to heal their patient's burns. The fractured femur was something else. Efforts to regenerate the nerves would take months, and were highly speculative at best.

The orthopedic surgeon located most of the bone fragments and, centimeter by arduous centimeter, achieved a reasonably good fit. Pins and metallic devices would be necessary to hold the delicate mechanism together. Fortunately, gangrene had not set in, but there were ugly indications the infection had spread and, unless brought under control swiftly, could easily become gangrenous. When they emerged from the theater, the eight doctors and their nurses were exhausted.

6

"What's today?"

"November first."

"Allah, I've been unconscious for a month?"

"A little more," Turhan said.

"What happened? I remember seeing a bright flash of light."

"You really don't want to know the details."

"I recall Halide wafting in and out of my dreams."

"She's been here to see you at five every afternoon. Doctor Ermenek arranged a teaching position for her at Robert College. The girls adore her. She's staying with the Ermeneks."

"What about you?"

"Ihsan was very understanding. He attached me to *Isharet's* Istanbul bureau for however long I want to stay. We've become the third largest newspaper in the country, next only to *Hürriyet* and *Milliyet*! Ihsan says thanks to me he's become a very wealthy man. And you, my friend, provided me with a wonderful exclusive story."

"What do you mean?"

"You're a celebrity. The sultan's ailing government cooperated fully with the nationalists to give aid to one of the heroes of the Sakarya. Doctors from all over treated you at the university. The first operation took ten hours. Since then, they've done two others to clean you up, or whatever it is doctors do."

"I itch dreadfully."

"You should. You had serious burns over more than half your body. The doctors tell me you're healing nicely and that the worst of the itching is over. Now that you're back in our world, the doctors are looking forward to the beginning of the real work."

"How so?"

"You're very lucky to have the lower part of your body intact. Even more fortunate to have two legs, although if I were you, I wouldn't bother to look down at one of them. You broke everything possible in the upper half of your right leg."

"*Mashallah,* my leg itches, too."

"Let's hope that's genuine feeling, Nadji. Men who've undergone amputations often feel pain where the leg used to be."

"Oh, there's no problem. I'll lift my leg to prove it."

The sheet didn't move. After a minute of trying, Nadji turned pale. Turhan looked away. He didn't want Nadji to see his own expression.

Shortly afterward, Doctor Ermenek made his rounds. Nadji was badly shaken by the realization his leg was not working at all. The doctor appeared to take this in stride. "Young man, you've been semi-conscious for more than a month. You've been lying around here like a piece of *pastırma* in the spice bazaar. Now you're upset because you can't jump up and run three kilometers the instant you wake up? You've got a lot of work ahead of you, Nadji. You're damned lucky. First, you can see. Second, your skin will most likely return to normal. And third, we've saved your life and your leg. It's up to you to make it work."

Then, more gently, he said, "But I'm glad you're with us, boy. Let me try something. Close your eyes, please."

Nadji did as he was told. The doctor lifted the blanket off his patient's right leg. "Tell me if you feel anything."

A nurse brought him a piece of ice, which he applied to the bottom of Nadji's right foot. "Allah! That's cold!"

"Good." remarked the doctor. He took out a small hammer and tapped the bottom of the same foot. "Now?"

"I feel a tapping on my heel," Nadji replied.

"Good." Doctor Ermenek removed a fork shaped instrument from his breast pocket and scratched along his patient's calf.

"I feel a very slight irritation on my right lower leg."

"Excellent," Doctor Ermenek replied, breathing an audible sigh and covering the leg. "You may open your eyes now. Nadji, I'm greatly relieved. Although our instruments showed there was some regeneration of nerves, we couldn't be sure unless we conducted tests when you were fully awake. I'll report this to my colleagues. I can't promise anything, but what just occurred is a good sign. A very good sign indeed."

During the next several weeks, while the "very good signs" increased, Nadji became increasingly impatient, then frustrated. It was three weeks before he could move the covers at all when he tried to lift his right leg. He labored six hours a day in physical therapy, lifting first one pound, then five, finally twenty pound weights with it. The itching abated. Slowly, stiffly, painfully, he was able to put the slightest weight on the leg. The following week, the doctor allowed him to put a bit more on it. Turhan and Halide took turns wheeling him to the hospital's pool. By year's end, Nadji found it possible to hobble around the ward on crutches.

"I'm glad to see you're making such splendid progress, Lieutenant. It seems all Istanbul has been praying for your recovery."

"I'm sorry. I don't believe we've met."

"Hükümdar, Abbas Hükümdar. Internal Security Police. You probably don't recognize me out of uniform." Nadji's visitor smiled easily. "We met in winter of 1918 near Sultanahmet."

The name and face were vaguely familiar. Then he remembered. *My God, he was there the night Halide was raped. He saw my shame. He must know the guilt I bear like a stone weight.*

As if sensing Nadji's discomfort. the man continued smoothly. "That was long ago, my friend," the man continued. "Times were hard. You've nothing to be ashamed of. You've proved yourself a brave man."

"You left a card that night. *Osmanli Kardeshlik*, the Ottoman Brotherhood," Nadji said.

"You've an excellent memory, Lieutenant."

Why is he here? Why now? Did Allah send him as a symbol to show He brought me such pain and suffering so I might atone for that night?

"I'll get right to the point, Lieutenant Akdemir. You're one of the few genuine, apolitical heroes in this war. We know you graduated from the Nationalist Military Academy. We're also aware you were discharged from the Ottoman Academy for nothing more than guilt by association. What do you *really* think of the Greeks, Lieutenant?" the man asked, abruptly switching to another subject.

"Excuse me, Hükümdar Effendi. I feel a bit stiff. Would you mind terribly if we walk for a little while. My doctor said I should get as much exercise as possible."

"But of course."

Nadji, using a cane to assist him, hobbled down the hall to the solarium. The man's question troubled him. What *did* he really think of the Greeks? They were the enemy, at least in this war. But they'd lived in Turkey for as long as he could remember. They paid taxes, accepted their position as a minority. He could not remember any individual Greek who'd wished him ill will. They were human beings. Two photographs jumped into his line of vision. A small, dark-haired woman with a serious face, standing alone. A small, dark-haired woman with a serious face, flanked on each side by a little girl with braided hair. *Nikos Stamoulatos, twenty-three, school teacher.* Nadji bit down hard on his lower lip as he felt the choking sensation, knew the tears were not far behind. His visitor's words interrupted his thoughts. By concentrating on them, he tried to quiet the insistent echo in his head, *Nikos Stamoulatos, twenty-three, school teacher.*

"Of course, you've only seen the Greek army from afar, so you wouldn't know whether they're like us or not."

Nikos Stamoulatos, twenty-three, school teacher. Dear Mrs. Stamoulatos, it is my sad duty to inform you that your husband...

"Take my word for it. They don't think like us. I was raised dirt poor in the Sultanahmet slums. My father slaved for them, got a pittance for his efforts, and died physically and spiritually broken at an early age. A good Turk could never compete with any of them. They'll always be foreigners. They spit on us behind our backs. You can never trust any foreigner. They're only out to undermine our motherland."

When they got to the solarium, Nadji sat down and stared out the window. Everything was gray. The Bosphorous, the sky, the snow-and-mud covered hills of Asiatic Istanbul. Mostly his spirit.

Hükümdar took a seat nearby. "Do you know anything about the Ottoman Brotherhood?"

Nadji shook his head. He had no idea where this conversation was leading, but he was becoming impatient.

"Very few people do. There are thirty of us. We try to keep out of the public eye."

"What does this have to do with me?"

"The Brotherhood is a very special, self-perpetuating secret society, pledged to purify the Turkish race by ridding it of foreign elements. You'd be surprised at the power we wield in our homeland. We number among our members the Deputy Secretary to the Grand Vizier and the Assistant Minister of the Interior." Hükümdar mentioned other names. Each man occupied a post of immense power and prestige, either in the Ottoman government or within the Nationalist hierarchy. "They're grooming us to take over in the years ahead."

"I don't understand what you're getting at."

"I told you we were self-perpetuating. We're looking for a very few younger men of proven leadership capacity. As I said, we've observed you for some time. We think you'd honor yourself and the Brotherhood by joining our number."

"You know my loyalties are to the Ankara government."

"Your present loyalties do not concern us. The Brotherhood doesn't care who's in *nominal* power, here or anywhere else in Turkey. We are the power *behind* the power."

"And if the government officials don't believe in your goals?"

"It doesn't matter what they believe. They're only in authority so long as *we* want them to be."

There was a cold ruthlessness in the man's manner that made Nadji nervous. He shifted uncomfortably in his chair. "I'm not sure I like what I hear."

Hükümdar stood up. His face reddened. "You're a fool, Akdemir! You dare question the opportunity of a lifetime? Go ahead, then, associate with drug dealers and arms smugglers like your journalist friend, Turhan, and see where *that* gets you!"

Impossible. Turhan? Now this fellow's gone too far.

"Why not confront your friend?" Hükümdar continued, his voice becoming more strident with each word. "Ask him about the Agha Khorusun, or, better yet, the Agha Nikrat? Then imagine what it would do to your budding career if it became known that you associated with someone of such a questionable past."

"I don't believe you!" Nadji rose and started hobbling toward his room as rapidly as he could. "I've known Turhan for... You're crazy! I'll not listen to such slander!"

"Oh, you think it's slander, do you, my fine young lieutenant?" the policeman shouted as he pursued Nadji down the corridor. "Don't forget, Akdemir, it's my job to know such things. I challenge Turhan to deny the charges. Let me fill you in on some of the sordid details of your friend's early life..."

"You know, Turhan, I know precious little about your childhood."

"What's to tell, Nadji? Diyarbakır, the caravan, lycée."

"And the Agha Nikrat?"

Turhan blanched, bit his lower lip, and stared straight ahead. "What about the Agha Nikrat?"

"Do you know what it could do to my career if the authorities learned of your past?"

"What do you mean? What *exactly* do you mean, Nadji?" Turhan asked hotly.

"You were involved with the Agha Nikrat. And the Agha Khorusun before him. Dealing in drugs. Smuggling arms to the Greeks."

Turhan rose, went to the window, stared out. When he looked back at Nadji, he said quietly, "I did not 'deal in drugs,' and I most certainly never questioned my associates about weapons of any kind."

"You deny you paid for your early days in Istanbul from money you made running errands for the caravan master Ibrahim? For the aghas?"

"I don't deny it at all. How else do you think I could have stayed alive in the capital?"

"Then you *did* deal in drugs."

"I ran *errands*. I owed loyalties. Without my friends, I'd have been nothing. If you're asking me if I'm ashamed of what I did, the answer's *no*, Nadji. I did what I had to do to stay alive, to fight a corrupt elite that thought no more of me than a pile of manure in the street!"

Their voices were sharp and brittle. "Damn you, Turhan! If the generals found out your background, my career'd be finished before it got started."

"Oh, *excuse me*, my Pasha!" Turhan roared. "How amazingly easy it is for you to find fault with others! You're the son of a general, the grandson of two colonels. When have you ever had to fight for a goddam thing in your life? You've had it all handed to you on a silver spoon. Military academy, commission, the security of a mansion in Shishli at a time when I waited on tables to eat. *Just who the hell do you think you are to tell me how to live*? I suppose you think I hang around you for the *influence* I might gain? Or that I'm trying to climb the rungs of society on your back, great hero?"

"You're not answering my question. Did you or did you not deal in drugs?"

"I've answered your question, and if you don't like my answer, you can shove it up your oh-so-clean arse! Yes, I made deliveries to the Agha's friends. And yes, I knew what I was delivering. Don't judge me by your standards, Nadji! What *you* were or what *you've* done in the past is none of my concern. I am what I am *today*, and I'll be damned if you or anyone else is going to question the way I got here!"

"I think you'd better go," Nadji said, stonily.

"Yes, perhaps I should.

Nadji was still in the hospital in January, 1922, when his family and friends prepared a celebration for his twentieth birthday. Turhan was conspicuously absent. After they'd cut the cake and sang birthday songs, Omer Akdemir hugged his son tightly and handed him two gifts. The first was wrapped in red tissue. "This is from the Gazi, who sent his regrets he couldn't come." Nadji unwrapped the paper carefully and opened what appeared to be a small jewelry case. Inside was a battered chrome watch, its chain still intact. There was a short message, written in Kemal's hand, "Dear Nadji: At the battle of Gelibolu, this watch saved my life. It has been a good friend in war. So have you. M.K."

"I've another gift as well." He handed his son a set of captain's insignia, a medal, and two parchment certificates. The first conferred on Nadji Akdemir the rank of *Kolagasi*, Captain, in the Turkish Republican army. The second awarded Captain Nadji Akdemir the Grand National Assembly's Medal of Valor for service to his nation, above and beyond the call of duty. It was signed by Gazi Mustafa Kemal, President of the Turkish Republic.

"Now I've got a surprise for all of you," Nadji said.

He rose slowly from the bed, pulled himself up until he was propped by the bed railing, and said, "Remember when they said I might never walk again?"

He put his cane aside and took one cautious step forward. Then another. The assembly buzzed excitedly as he reached out to take his third step. The spasm came like a thunderbolt, and he collapsed in a heap at their feet, screaming in pain.

"Go away. I don't want to see anybody." His voice was muffled, the covers pulled over his head. He'd turned toward the wall.

"Don't you think you're acting childish, Nadji. Sooner or later you'll have to face me or suffocate," Halide insisted.

"Maybe that's the best thing," he mumbled miserably.

"Suit yourself. Running away from the problem's not going to make it any better. Besides, it's awfully hard to run when you haven't even tried to help your legs. You sat in a wheelchair, then you walked with a cane. Then, when you thought you were ready, you stumbled and fell. And after all that work, just because you fell once, you simply felt sorry for yourself and gave up."

"That's a low, cheap thing to say!" he shouted angrily, emerging from under the covers and glaring at her. "You of all people know what it's like…"

"Oh I do, do I?" she blazed back. "What do you mean, Nadji Akdemir? What *exactly* do you mean? Do you mean my hunchback? Or the fact that I was raped? Just *which* indignity do you think is the greatest, mine or yours? I couldn't do anything about mine. You *can*, but you *won't* do anything about yours! *What have you suffered that's so great you have any right to tell me what I can or cannot say?*"

"My paralysis is Allah's punishment for taking you to Stamboul that night. For standing by and watching helplessly as you were – violated.

I knew I'd be punished for it sooner or later. Nothing in life happens without consequence."

Halide was thoughtful for several moments. When she spoke, her tone was calm, measured. "That 'violation' was a crime against me, Nadji, not you. As for my punishment, what sin could I have committed before my birth which led to my deformity? If there's nothing any of us can do about what happens, why bother to have doctors or teachers or scientists?

"Some things can't be changed. They happen for reasons we can't understand. If you really want to talk about why I was raped – I'm not afraid to use that word – we must go back to when I fell in love with Metin Ermenek. I would never have come to Turkey but for him. Whom do I blame for his death? The Turks? The Allies? Myself? Did the fact we made love the night before he died cause him to momentarily forget where he was? To take a risk he'd not otherwise have taken? Did you volunteer to take me to Stamboul that night? Or did you go at my insistence?

"I've come to grips with things I can't change. Long ago, I forgave Allah for the way I was born. I forgave Allah for taking Metin Ermenek from me. I refuse to accept my rape as punishment for Metin's death. I was raped, Nadji. Plain and simple. You didn't do it, you didn't cause it, and there was nothing you could do to prevent it. My body was violated. My soul remains my own. Put what happened behind you, my friend. I have.

"When there's something I *can* change and I don't *try, then* I invite Allah's retribution. And when there's something you *can* change and *you* don't try, I cannot forgive you that. There's nothing wrong with your legs. You've convinced yourself you'll never walk again. Would you have survived Sakarya with such an attitude? The evening I met you, I gave you a gift, do you remember?"

"An engraved marble paperweight that said 'Nadji Akdemir, Pasha.'"

"That's right. I placed my faith in you. I believed in you. I still believe in you. I can forgive you almost anything. But if you let me down and cause me to have wasted the francs I spent on that gift, I will never forgive you!"

For the first time in weeks, he smiled. Then, uncontrollably, he started to cry, the emotions of years finally tearing away from his soul.

Halide continued to visit him daily.

Physically, Nadji improved. Emotionally, he felt a great emptiness. There were times when, inexplicably, he couldn't sleep at night.

Abbas Hükümdar came by on two more occasions. Nadji finally convinced Abbas he would not join the Ottoman Brotherhood. The policeman's visits abruptly terminated.

One day, Halide was just about leave when, for no reason she could discern, Nadji started shaking uncontrollably. "Are you all right?"

"Yes. No. I don't know, Halide."

"Would you like me to stay a while?"

"Please."

She sat in silence for as few moments. "I've spoken recently to Turhan."

"I have nothing to say."

"He's as badly hurt as you. Remember a couple of months ago when I talked about forgiveness?"

"How can I forgive him after what he concealed from me?"

Halide gazed steadily at him. When she spoke, she chose her words carefully. "He said almost the same thing, Nadji. He feels you betrayed the friendship by failing to accept him for what he is."

"He consorted with drug dealers and gun-runners."

"Are you such a saint that you've never sinned?"

"You said what happened wasn't my fault."

"That's not what I asked, Nadji. Let me tell you a little bit about Turhan Türkoğlu. The Turhan you think you know. The one you don't know at all."

For the next half-hour, Halide told Nadji the story of her friend Turhan. About a small village in southeast Turkey and a boy who tried to save the life of his Armenian teacher in the name of friendship. About a young man who sat watch for hour after sleepless hour to bring a deformed young woman back from the grave after her fiancé had been killed, in the name of friendship. About an out-of-work reporter who risked his life to right a wrong being done to two strangers in a dark alley in Sultanahmet on a winter night when Turks were without rights in their own capital.

And at the end, when Nadji was openly, unashamedly weeping, she squeezed his hand. "Do you think he'll ever forgive me, Halide?"

"Why don't you telephone him. Invite him here and see."

"What if he refuses to accept my call?"

"That's a chance you'll have to take, my friend. When you were just starting on the road to recovery, the first step was the hardest, and took the greatest amount of courage. Try and take another first step, Nadji. I can't think of two other people who'd better deserve the happiness that call would bring."

Next day, Nadji redoubled his efforts. If the physical therapist wanted him to work for an hour, he willed himself to work for two. Within six months after his birthday, less than a year after his injury,

Nadji walked with only a slight limp. His body had filled out. All hint of boyishness was gone. Other than that slight limp, no one would ever have known that the incident near Polatli had happened. Or that he and Turhan had ever quarreled.

7

Nadji returned to Ankara on July 1, 1922, amazed at the changes a year had wrought. New buildings rose everywhere throughout the valley. The capital was now a substantial city. The Gazi, Mustafa Kemal, occupied a spacious pink house on Chankaya hill, overlooking the capital. A community of villas adjoined his home. Nadji's parents were ensconced in one of them. Most of the ladies on Chankaya hill appeared in public unveiled, in the nationalist fashion. One day, Mustafa Kemal invited Nadji to his residence. It was furnished in comfortable, if heavy, Germanic style, with leather armchairs, Turkish carpets on every floor, and a collection of arms on the walls.

His father, General Omer Akdemir, was there when Nadji entered Kemal's office. "Captain," the Gazi said. "The time has come for our army to make a final stand and rid our motherland of foreign forces. I'm meeting with officers of every rank. While the ultimate decision must be mine, I solicit your suggestions as to where our final assault should take place."

For the next hour, the three men studied a large, three dimensional map of Anatolia spread on a table adjacent to the Gazi's modern desk, which contained red and blue flags showing troop concentrations, garrisons and strongholds.

"Well?" Mustafa Kemal asked.

"Gazi," Nadji said. "The Greek forces are stretched over a three hundred mile front from the Sea of Marmara to the Menderes Valley. Their strong points are at Eskishehir in the north and Afyon in the south. If I were the Greek general, I'd expect a Turkish attack to come against Eskishehir, since we have our largest concentration of forces in that area. The Greeks would hardly expect us to attack Afyon, their most heavily fortified position. Afyon commands the direct supply line to Izmir. If we could knock out the strongest Greek position, our advance might be limitless."

The Gazi stood up, moved around to the map table. He stared down at the map for several minutes, without a word. When he looked up, it was as though the other men in the room had intruded on his private thoughts. "Very well, Captain. Thank you for your thoughts. You may take your leave."

Less than a fortnight later, Nadji returned to the pink house. His father, Kemal and a short, mild-looking man with sparse hair and a thin moustache, were present when he arrived at the Gazi's office. "Captain, this is my Chief of Staff, Ismet Pasha, who now calls himself Ismet Inönü," Kemal said. "Ismet, Captain Akdemir is the young man I told you about. His ideas were – interesting."

He turned to the group. "Be seated, gentlemen. Let's have tea." He clapped his hands. A steward brought a silver tray with a sterling teapot, four crystal glasses and a large plate of sweets.

"When I was fighting the final battles of the war against the Allies," Kemal said, "I was impressed by Allenby's campaign in Palestine. He recognized surprise was an essential element of a successful battle plan.

We are going to attack the main Greek forces at Afyon and astonish them. During the next month, we'll withdraw the necessary troops from the north and move them east of Dumlupinar. We'll make all our movements at night. During daylight, the soldiers will rest in villages and under shade trees. They'll spread out as much as possible, to be invisible to the enemy's air reconnaissance. Those remaining behind will light extra campfires near Eskishehir each night, so it'll look like we're massing to take that city.

"General Akdemir, you'll be in charge of the northern ruse. Ismet, you'll supervise the movement of troops in place. Captain, you'll act as liaison between the northern and southern commands."

"And you, *Gazi*?" Ismet asked.

"I'll be where I belong. Commanding the front."

At 8:00 PM, August 25, 1922, all communications between Anatolia and the outside world suddenly ceased. Telegrams went unanswered. All telephone circuits were inexplicably busy. The last trains of the evening between Istanbul and Ankara had departed and were enroute to their destinations. The railroad station at Ankara had closed for the night.

Outside Eskishehir, troops lit more fires than usual. For the first time in months, cannons rumbled as the Turks lobbed a few shells into the Greek lines. The Greek commander, General Hajianestis, was settling in to sleep on his yacht in Smyrna harbor, which the Turks called Izmir, when he learned of the assault. He believed the attack would burn itself out by daybreak, but just in case, he ordered a large contingent of troops to proceed north from Afyon as insurance.

That night, Kemal quietly moved his headquarters to a camp just outside Afyon. His troops marched into position on the slopes under cover of darkness. An hour before dawn the Greeks, many of whom were sleeping off the effects of a party in Afyon the night before, suddenly awakened to the thunderous roar of an artillery barrage. Kemal's orders were short and to the point: "Soldiers, your goal is the sea!"

During the next five days Turkish forces mowed down the enemy. They overran Hellenic defense positions within twelve hours of the first shot. A week later, Izmit, Afyon, and Eskishehir fell to the nationalist forces. Half the Greek army had been captured or slain. The remaining troops fled in disarray toward the coast. In their frustration, Constantine's surviving soldiers burned and looted villages, raped any female over the age of nine they could find, and trampled the crops. If the Turks could not be beaten, they'd be given cause to remember who had been here.

The government in Athens asked Britain to arrange a truce that would at least preserve Greek rule in Izmir. The Gazi refused to even talk about it. One by one, the Greek bastions fell, Aydin, Balikesir, Bursa. The Greeks razed Manisa, then continued their disorderly retreat toward the Aegean. Constantine's government resigned. By September 7, the Dardanelles and the Sea of Marmara were under Turkish control. It was a lightning victory, unparalleled in Turkish history. The war rapidly approached its climax.

Thousands of Greek soldiers and peasants flooded into Izmir from all over Anatolia. Fifty thousand Greek soldiers, civil servants, and police boarded a convoy of warships and sailed for Athens, leaving behind a like number of prisoners of war, and uncounted Greek peasants. By September 9, Izmir was in nationalist hands.

The following day, Gazi Mustafa Kemal, wearing a plain Turkish uniform with neither insignia nor badges, drove into Izmir at the head of a procession of open cars decked with olive branches. He went directly to *konak*, the government building on the quay, which had been Greek headquarters. A large Greek flag was spread like a carpet on its steps. Kemal said Greek national pride had suffered enough. He refused to walk on the blue and white banner, and ordered its removal.

8

Kemal scheduled a formal dinner celebrating the Turkish entry into Izmir for September 13. The guest list included Hamdi Ülker, the distinguished Turkish statesman who'd been instrumental in negotiating the recent Turkish-French accords, and his wife.

"Gazi," Ülker remarked to Kemal, "might I beg a small favor of you?"

"It never hurts to ask, Effendim."

"My daughter, Aysheh, is home from the university in Bologna for a month. She's nineteen and has never attended a state social event. Would it be possible for her to attend this one? I assure you the child will not disgrace your table."

"Of course, my friend. Not only that, but," his blue eyes sparkled, "I've got a dinner companion in mind for her."

Less than five hours before the scheduled event, Mustafa Kemal spoke with his old friend, General Akdemir. "Omer," he said, "I'd like to have Nadji attend the state dinner this evening."

"You make it sound more like a command than an invitation. What have you in mind?"

"Hamdi Ülker's daughter has no escort for the event..."

Akdemir laughed out loud. "Rest assured the boy will be there."

That evening, Nadji entered the Izmir Palas hotel attired in his finest dress whites. The tall, brown-haired young man, with wide shoulders and slender waist, was the picture of what Kemal wished to present to the world as the new face of Turkey. He was extraordinarily handsome, with close-cropped, stylish moustache, clear green eyes and an engaging, open smile. He wore several military decorations, including the Grand National Assembly medallion. More than a few women noticed him as he strode through the hotel's entryway.

He thought about the conversation that had brought him here. "Father, why would the Gazi want me at the event? The most important people in Izmir have been invited. I'm a mere captain."

"Don't ask me, Nadji. I'm just passing on the invitation."

Nadji was discreetly directed to a velvet-lined elevator, which whisked him to the top floor of the hotel. As he walked into the room, looking for his father, he heard the Gazi's voice. "And this is Captain Nadji Akdemir, the young man I told you about." But she was all he saw.

Grey-violet eyes. Allah! I've never seen that color. His only conscious impression was of huge, incredibly beautiful eyes. Then she spoke. Her voice was warm and throaty.

"The hero of Polatlı. The man who forced the old and new governments of Turkey to cooperate, while we prayed for his recovery. I'm glad to meet you, Captain." The apparition smiled. She had even, white teeth. Thick, luxuriant, honey-colored hair fell in soft waves to her shoulders, surrounding the most beautiful face he'd ever seen. And stunning grey-violet eyes.

The look on Nadji's face was not lost on Kemal, who impishly said, "I'm afraid, Aysheh *Hanım*, our hero has momentarily lost his voice.

Kolagasi Nadji," he said. "May I present Miss Aysheh Ülker, daughter of our government's ambassador-designate to the United States of America."

Nadji reached out, took Aysheh's hand and bowed. "Miss Ülker, please pardon my oafishness. I am dazzled."

The girl was well aware of the effect she had on men. They often tried pompously or dismissively to disguise their feelings in her presence, but the message came through. This young man's candor was certainly an appealing change. And he really was quite handsome.

"I'm flattered," she replied, flashing that incredible smile again. The girl wore no makeup and needed none. Her face was oval-shaped with clear, translucent skin, emphasized by the simple, high-necked black gown she wore. She was a head shorter than Nadji. "Would the captain care to escort me to dinner?" she asked. Again that caressing voice. He offered her his arm. When she took it, he felt dizzy. Somehow, he reached the table without tripping over himself. Footmen held out their chairs.

Dinner conversation centered on the great offensive that had brought the army to Izmir. Kemal reminisced, the *raki* having loosened his tongue. "Indeed," he said, "Omer Pasha on my north flank, Ismet on my south, the gallant young captain racing between them." Nadji blushed deeply.

"Twice a hero," his lovely dinner companion said. "I'm impressed."

"Believe me, it was nothing, Miss Ülker," he volunteered clumsily. *Stupid boor, he thought, can't you say something with a shred of intelligence?*

"Why not call me Aysheh?"

"It would be my honor Miss, uh, Aysheh." *Say something, idiot. Anything. Anything at all. You don't want to lose her.* "I, uh, understand your father is being posted to America." *Good, idiot. Now see if you can put two sentences together before she gets up and walks away.* "Have you been there as well?"

"No, I'm afraid not. The farthest I've been is Italy."

"Oh." *Wonderful, you ass. What a brilliant statement.* "What were you doing there, Miss Aysheh?"

"I spent last year at the University in Bologna, studying the history of western civilization."

Wonderful. You could not know less about anything. "I'm afraid my education is sadly lacking. I've traveled throughout Turkey, but my training has been at the military academy. I've learned much about *Turkish* history, but I profess my ignorance of the rest of the world."

He's like a little boy, she thought. Charming, really.

"Tell me about Bologna," he said, conversation becoming a little – not much – easier.

"Except for the university, which goes back seven hundred years, it's not very old by Turkish standards. Bologna's just another big city. But it's not far from Venice, and *that's* a city like none other. The only two ways to get around are by gondola through the canals, or on foot over the hundreds of bridges. It's such a romantic place. It reminds me a little bit of Istanbul."

"Do you miss your family when you're away?"

"Yes, but I've learned to live with that. Father will probably have several overseas postings now that it appears the nationalists will govern Turkey, and Mother will undoubtedly go with him. My older sister, Talya, is married with two children and lives in Istanbul. I may not see much of her either. Somehow I'll have to learn to fend for myself."

Not if I can help it, Nadji thought.

"You know," she continued, "one of my favorite places when I was growing up was Ephesus. I haven't been there in years. It's less than a day's journey. Would you think me very forward if I asked you to escort me to the ruins? I'm leaving for Italy in three weeks. I'd so love to see it again."

The captain blushed and was about to answer when they heard shouting immediately outside the room. The door burst open and a dark-haired little man said, "Gazi, ladies and gentlemen. You must vacate the hotel. Izmir is on fire!"

As he rushed to the window, Nadji saw Güzel Izmir – beautiful Izmir – burning with an eerie, copper-colored light. "I think," Omer Akdemir said to his son, "we should escort the guests to safety. The elevator's probably jammed with panicked people trying to get out of this building. Look for a stairway."

Nadji found the unused exit, went swiftly back to the room, secured his cloak, and sought out Aysheh. "Miss Ülker," he said. "We must evacuate immediately. Please take my coat with you for protection. It's bound to be chilly in the night air. You can return it when next we meet." He directed the senior Ülkers toward the staircase. "Please go ahead," he said. "I'll gather the others. I wanted you to go first, so you wouldn't be lost in the crush." Aysheh smiled at him with frank appreciation. After he saw them safely descend, he went into the city to do what he could to help. As it happened, that was precious little indeed.

Although Turks, Greeks and Armenians all blamed one another, no one ever found out how the first blaze started. As the inferno spread, looters and Turkish soldiers, settling old scores, started other fires throughout the city. The fire brigade discovered to its horror that all the city's fire hoses had been cut and the water cisterns emptied.

Ismet, who'd left the party and was now in command, declared that the Greeks had planned to burn the city as their parting "gift" to the conquering Turkish army. Within two hours, flames spread to the waterfront, driving inhabitants and refugees toward the sea.

Immediately after he reported to the Turkish command post, Nadji went to Konak hospital. He directed soldiers to bring the sick and aged down to the safety of the harbor on improvised stretchers, and made over a fifty such trips himself. Bewildered people, their eyes glazed, huddled in the streets. Just after midnight, the entire line of houses along the waterfront caught fire all at once. Crowds surged away from the burning houses in panic. Their screams were louder than the crackling flames.

When a rumor spread that Turkish machine gunners were blocking each end of the quay, bedlam erupted. Thousands of people, frightened out of their minds, wandered aimlessly about, many carrying flaming bundles. Nadji shouted that the rumor was false, but his voice was lost among the shrieks of terrified people, and the loud crack of wooden buildings collapsing. Towers of raging flame rose hundreds of feet into the air.

Every small craft in the harbor ferried people to ships anchored in the Bay. These vessels could not accommodate even half the terrified crush of humanity. Women threw their children into boats to save them. Men dove into the water. The strongest of them swam out to the warships. There were boats and bodies everywhere. It was impossible for the ships standing offshore to take on the thousands in the bay. Each gave priority to its own nationals. The others would somehow have to fend for themselves. Families crowded onto small fishing boats, pushing, shoving, overloading. Many flimsy vessels capsized. Their inhabitants drowned.

Men and women poured out of burning buildings onto Birinji Kordon. A woman in her mid-twenties burst out of a nearby apartment house, screaming hysterically, her dress afire. Nadji grabbed a blanket and pushed the woman to the ground, then rolled her in the wool cover, snuffing out the flames. "My baby!" the woman screamed, oblivious to her own pain. "My baby's still upstairs! She'll burn to death! I must go back!"

Nadji looked up and saw a young girl, about four years old, in the second story window of a building once removed from the inferno. It was obvious that within minutes, the fire would spread to the residence and consume the child. He ran over and grabbed a bystander. "We can't let that child die!" he shouted. "Help me!" The two raced over to the building. The middle-aged man who'd followed him grasped one end of the large blanket. Nadji seized the other. "Jump!" he shouted to the little girl.

"I can't. I'm afraid," she whimpered.

"Listen, darling," Nadji spoke calmly. "You won't get hurt. This man and I are holding the blanket. We won't let go. Just jump into it. You'll be all right."

"Promise?" she asked.

"My word of honor." His voice was strong and confident. The child, reassured, closed her eyes, pinched her nose with her thumb and forefinger and jumped. The youngster bounced lightly as she hit the blanket, then settled into the cover. Nadji hugged the little one and carried her to safety across the street. He turned to thank the man who'd helped him, but the fellow had disappeared.

As dawn broke, a new sound added the final touch of surrealism and ghastliness to this night in hell. According to custom, when the British fleet was in port, the flagship's naval band began each morning with a rousing serenade. Faithful to that tradition, musicians on board the British command vessel started playing bright, martial music, which mingled incongruously with the screams of the victims and the roar of the flames.

The sun rose. The wind abated. The fire died down. In a single night, twenty-five thousand buildings had been burned to the ground. The most beautiful Turkish city on the Aegean, Smyrna, was no more.

Miraculously, relatively few lives were lost. But the destruction of property was catastrophic. The western press quickly condemned the Turkish military for this final atrocity of the war.

A week after Smyrna was razed, Mustafa Kemal declared that a new western-style city – a wholly Turkish city – would rise from the ashes of Turkey's second metropolis. It would be more beautiful, more cohesive than before. It would truly be *Güzel* Izmir.

9

"Thank you so much for returning my cloak." It was all Nadji could say. He was tongue-tied again. She looked even more appealing by daylight than she had at night. For the past ten days, he'd commanded patrols clearing the harbor of rubble and debris. Though the evening of the thirteenth had ended as a nightmare, it had started with a dream. He couldn't get that dream out of his mind. Now she'd appeared again.

Aysheh wore a loose-fitting, tan summer dress that highlighted her every soft curve. Her lustrous hair cascaded over her shoulders. She seemed somehow smaller. As he glanced down, Nadji realized why. In place of the fashionable European high heeled shoes she'd worn that night, she was wearing flat sandals. Her legs were slender, as perfectly proportioned as the rest of her. She caught his admiring stare and teased, "When you've had enough of looking, would you care to listen to what I have to say?"

He blushed deeply. "I'm...I'm sorry, Miss Ülker...uh..."

"'Aysheh' will do very well. I seem to recall a dashing young captain who promised to take me to Ephesus. It's been ten days. I'm still waiting."

"Well, uh, Miss Ülker...Aysheh, I've been awfully busy since the fire and I had no idea where you lived, and..." the words came out in a fumbled rush.

"And you couldn't have found that information through the Gazi or your father?" she scolded, teasingly. "What if our home had been destroyed by the fire? Would you have tried to rescue me?"

"I didn't think. I'm sorry."

"Is that all you can say this morning? Nadji Akdemir, do you intend to take me to Ephesus or not?"

"You still want to go with me?"

"Do you think, Captain, that a young lady of my 'status'," she pirouetted gaily about, mocking herself, "would have come here simply to return a coat?"

"Well, uh, when did you have in mind that we go?"

"I'm in no hurry. You may requisition an automobile and pick me up tomorrow morning, promptly at nine," she said, with charming insouciance. "You needn't bother to pack a picnic lunch. I'll have one ready for us. I'll see you then, *Mon Capitain*." She was gone in the swish of a skirt. Nadji was befuddled, bemused, and more than a little in love.

That afternoon, General Omer Akdemir grumbled, "I suppose this is the wave of the future. 'Father, can I use the family car, I have an important engagement?' What do you expect the poor old man to say?"

"Try 'yes,' father?"

"Who's this 'important engagement' anyway? Someone I might know?"

"She was at the dinner party the night of the fire. Aysheh Ülker."

"Hamdi's daughter? Well, you have my permission, not that you'd need it, my blessing and, most important for your purposes, the keys to the car. Drive carefully."

"By the way, father. Have you any idea where the Ülkers live?"

Nadji was up before seven the following morning. He inspected the car to make certain every speck of dust was removed. His father had kept the aging Mercedes in mint condition. Although the odometer showed nearly one hundred ten thousand kilometers, the car's body gleamed as if it had just come from the factory. Nadji showered a long time, soaping often, taking advantage of the wonderful western amenities offered at his father's quarters. He'd applied talcum powder to his body, then shaved, cursing as the razor nicked his neck. Damn! He'd wanted to look absolutely perfect. He pondered for half an hour what he should wear. The military dress outfit looked so well on him. Yet it would be out of place on a picnic. Finally, he selected an open-necked brown shirt with matching western-style trousers. No good. A green shirt would much better bring out the color of his eyes. *Wonderful, Nadji, you're as fussy and vain as a woman.* In the end, he wore a plaid shirt with olive-colored slacks, and a light, civilian jacket.

He arrived at the fashionable suburb of Göztepe at eight forty-five, and sat impatiently in the car. After what seemed an eternity, he looked down at his watch. It must have stopped. Surely more than five minutes had gone by! Finally, it was four minutes to nine. Acceptable. As soon as he got to the front door, it swung open. "I was wondering if you were going to sit in the car the entire morning. Come in, Nadji, we're just finishing breakfast. My, don't you look the sporty one?" His senses were assailed by the delicate, flowery scent, the beauty of the young woman, and her wonderful, musical voice.

"Good morning Hamdi Effendim, Madame Ülker," Nadji said respectfully, bowing slightly.

"Good morning, Captain," the diplomat responded. "You'll take good care of our daughter, of course?" A smile crinkled the corners of his mouth. Hamdi Ülker had studied the young officer's dossier after the dinner party. What he'd seen had pleased him.

"Yes, Sir. If you'd like, there's plenty of room for you and Madame Ülker to come with us. If there's not enough food, I'd certainly be willing to stop enroute."

"Never mind, young man," Aysheh's mother answered sharply. "Hamdi has been promising for weeks he was going to sort out what things he intends to take to Washington."

"Come on, Nadji," Aysheh said. "My parents simply want to be alone." She bent down and kissed her mother, then stood on her tiptoes and bussed her father on the cheek. "We'll be back before nightfall."

"Drive carefully. Have a good time, children," Hamdi said, dismissing them.

Aysheh wore a summery yellow outfit. *She looks more beautiful every time I see her*, Nadji thought. In the two weeks since the party, Nadji had read everything he could get his hands on about Ephesus. Still, he relished the sound of her voice on the way down as she talked about the place. "Pompeii was a wealthy holiday town of twenty-five thousand when it was destroyed by Mount Vesuvius eighteen hundred years ago. Ephesus was the third largest city in the Roman Empire, ten times as large as Pompeii. It wasn't destroyed by a sudden catastrophe. It hung on for several hundred years until the Menderes River silted up its harbor. More than two hundred fifty thousand people lived in Ephesus during the time of the prophet Jesus."

"And today?"

"Less than five percent of the ruins have been uncovered."

They drove for three hours over the modern, two lane macadam highway. The hillsides were verdant with tea and tobacco plantations. At one point, they stopped to watch a small caravan, a dozen camels walking by the side of the road, each loaded with an assortment of commodities.

"They become scarcer each year," Nadji said. "As more roads are built and Turkey acquires more trucks, we'll see less and less of the old ways in Turkey. It's sad, really. I witnessed 'progress' in Ankara, during the past couple of years. When I first saw the place, it was a dusty, thirsty little town. Now, buildings have sprouted like weeds all over the place. There are more than a hundred thousand people, but the atmosphere I felt when I first arrived has disappeared."

"You mean the captain is a romantic?" she chided. "I thought that kind of thing was left to women."

"Not always. My father's a gentle man, but that gentleness comes from strength. When you're strong, confident in yourself, you can appreciate beauty and tenderness."

Shortly before noon, they reached Selchuk, from which a narrow road led to the ruins. Less than a mile off the main highway, Nadji stopped the car and pointed wordlessly up and to the right. The crenellated walls of a huge, ancient structure sat atop a large hill, five hundred feet above them.

"The Citadel," Aysheh said. "It's one of the best places from which to see Ephesus. Ready for a hike?"

Within a quarter hour, they'd scaled the heights of the butte. The view from the summit was worth the walk. The rocky bones of the ancient metropolis spread over a field several miles wide. "Behold, the Acropolis of Selchuk!" Aysheh announced proudly. "This part dates from the fall of the Roman Empire in the west. Successive conquerors built onto it for the next thousand years." As they entered the walls, she pointed out a huge, skeletal building. "Originally, this was the church of Saint John the Evangelist. The Christians say his tomb is somewhere under the building. Eventually, the place became a warehouse. Then, a hundred years ago, it was destroyed in an earthquake."

"Behold," Nadji responded, imitating her tone of voice, "the *lunch* which Nadji Akdemir carried up to the Acropolis of Selchuk!" He unfolded a blanket and they sat, contentedly eating *dolma* – stuffed grape leaves – cold sliced lamb, bread and pickled vegetables. Aysheh removed bottles of orange and apple juice from the hamper. Afterward, stretching out on the blanket, they stared up at an azure sky. Puffy clouds drifted lazily above them. Nadji felt a gentle tap on his shoulder. "Hey, my escort, you've dozed off. I thought I was more seductive than that."

"You are, Aysheh," he said, blushing. "It's just that it's so beautiful up here, the sun's so warm, and I felt so relaxed."

"Relaxed, are you? Well, Captain, how does this suit your idea of relaxation?" She leaned over and boldly kissed him on the mouth. The young man, caught with his guard down, responded vigorously. Before long they were stroking one another, kissing hungrily, passionately. They stopped, each breathless, shaken.

"Animal!" she said, winking. "Trying to take advantage of a sweet, innocent young maiden. Come on, we'd better see Ephesus before something happens that shouldn't." She grasped his hand and pulled him to his feet.

They descended to the valley below. After a short drive to the entrance of Ephesus, they walked along a street of pure, white marble, with columns, statues, and ruins and remnants of shops and houses everywhere.

When Nadji pulled out his pocket watch, he was startled to find it was three in the afternoon. "I know it's getting late," Aysheh said, "but I'd so like to stop at the small museum in Selchuk on the way back, if only for half an hour."

"Of course," he said, holding her hand and smiling down at her. "This has been the happiest day of my life."

She grinned and pressed back. "It certainly hasn't been the worst of mine."

The museum was small, but impressive. Each piece had been selected lovingly, by an educated hand. "There's something I'd like to show you, Nadji. However," she said, barely suppressing a giggle, "it's for men only." She pointed to a remote corner of the room. There was small, plain case, covered in wood, as if a new exhibit were going to be placed there, and it wasn't quite ready.

Nadji approached the case. A small, unobtrusive sign to the right of the exhibit read, "View what's inside the case only if you are not faint of heart." A miniature block and tackle was attached to the wood cover. Nadji pulled the rope. The cover lifted from the case. He looked inside briefly and immediately dropped the cover. There was no bang as the plywood walls dropped into place, coming to rest on a thick, rubber cushion. Whoever had planned the exhibit must have been aware of the shock it would cause. He looked across the room. Aysheh convulsed with laughter. Slowly, hypnotized by what he'd seen, he lifted the wooden casing again and stared.

A small, terra cotta statuette, eight inches tall and two thousand years old, grinned back at him. The little fellow's penis, as long as the statue was tall, pointed straight out and up. A sign inside the case, at the foot of the statue read, "The mischievous little god *Besh*. In the days of the Roman empire, prostitution was a prevalent and socially accepted part of daily life. The small statue you see above 'pointed out' the way to where such entertainment could be found."

When Nadji lowered the cover a second time and looked back, Aysheh was in animated conversation with a spry gentleman of seventy. He crossed the room to them. "Nadji," Aysheh said, "I'd like you to meet one of my favorite people in the world, Professor Ismail Dora. Uncle Ismail taught anthropology and archaeology at Istanbul University. Professor, this is my friend, Captain Nadji Akdemir. Professor Dora's known me since..."

"Since before you were born, my dear. We don't speak of that, since it would age me even more. I'm pleased to meet you, Captain. Might I suggest since it's getting quite late to be driving home, you consider spending the night here? My home has several extra rooms. I'll telephone Ambassador Ülker to make sure it's all right. It'll give me an excuse to talk with Hamdi."

Nadji and Aysheh smiled at one another. "Would you mind terribly, Uncle Ismail?" Aysheh asked.

"Of course not."

He returned some minutes later, a smile lighting up his features. "All arranged," he said. "Tomorrow when you return to Izmir, you'll have a passenger. Hamdi's invited me to spend the week there."

Although Professor Dora was a widower, his studies kept him far from lonely. His cook and housekeeper, a woman from Selchuk village, cared for him as if he were a child. After dinner, Dora suggested the three of them sit outside on his porch, to take advantage of the lovely evening breeze. His house was located on a rise above the ruins. Nadji and Aysheh watched as the sun set in the west, lighting the pillars and marble roads with a red-golden fire similar to, but much kinder than, the one they'd experienced in Izmir two weeks before. They sat together on a double swinging couch suspended from the roof. Their host sat on a bentwood rocker. For the next hour, they listened as he told them of his life in the now defunct Empire. Aysheh leaned lightly against Nadji and held his hand in hers. He shivered despite the warmth of the early autumn evening. He felt as though someone were tickling him inside, and found it hard to concentrate on what Professor Dora was saying.

At length, the professor stood up, stretched, and said, "It's easy for young people to stay up 'til all hours. Not so for an old fellow like me. Each of your rooms is off the dining room. Your beds are turned down and ready. I'll leave a lamp burning in the house to light your way. Don't stay up too late."

Nadji and Aysheh sat in silence for awhile, holding hands and rocking. A full moon had risen in the east. They looked down at the remains of the city, which had turned silvery white. They kissed, tenderly at first, then passionately, taking up where they'd left off that afternoon. Soon kissing would not be enough. Aysheh broke loose and jumped to her feet. "Come on," she said, her voice strained and husky, "let's go see Ephesus by night."

It took them ten minutes to find their way down the hill, into the ghost city. Alternating shadows and lustrous bright spots created by moon and marble made the place a magical wonderland. Nadji led the way down a narrow avenue until they came to a wide marble road. The shells of the ancient stores provided a sheltered covering. He turned to speak to his lovely companion. Aysheh was gone. At first, he thought she'd simply stopped to look at one of the pillars or a small building near by. Then he became concerned.

"Aysheh," he called softly.

There was no reply. He called again, this time with greater force. Still no response. Nadji heard a slight, shuffling noise twenty yards away. He started over to investigate the sound, then stopped dead in his tracks. Aysheh emerged from the shadows wearing a wonderfully inviting smile. And nothing else.

Nadji's breath caught in his throat. She was the most heart-stoppingly dazzling creature he'd ever seen. She crooked her finger, signaling him to come to her. He moved stiffly, woodenly, in a trance. Aysheh stood as still as an alabaster statue of Venus. In his eyes, the goddess of love would have wept in frustration had she stood in competition with this maiden.

"Aysheh?"

"Years from now, when our children's children are grown, look at me then, and remember me as I am at this moment."

The apparition was gone. Moments later, she was clothed. They walked in loving silence back to Professor Dora's home, amidst the music of a thousand crickets.

On July 24, 1923, after months of the most difficult negotiations, Turkey and the Allies signed the Treaty of Lausanne. Having earned its right to do so, Turkey came to the bargaining table as an equal. The integrity of the Turkish nation was preserved. The war was finally over.

That same week, under a canopy of flowers, Nadji Akdemir's dream came true. Aysheh Ülker, changed her name to his. That night, they did not listen to the sound of crickets, nor the orchestra serenading them beneath their bedroom window. They made exquisite music of their own.

PART FOUR:

HEROES 1928–1937

1

In spring, 1928, Halide's father, Yujel Orhan died in his sleep. The years since the Great War had been good to him. He'd found happiness in his marriage to Françoise, who had died the year before. Due to a series of fortunate investments, Yujel had become a wealthy man. His entire estate went to Halide. With her beloved father gone, Halide's ties to France receded. At Omer Akdemir's suggestion, she purchased a large home, which she jokingly called the "Belgrade Palas," in the Belgrade Forest, several miles north of Istanbul. She transferred the remainder of her funds to Switzerland for security.

The Ottoman Empire was now a memory. The last sultan had been deposed and retired to San Remo. The caliph – the Islamic religious leader – had been banished to Geneva. After putting down a revolt in Kurdistan, and divorcing his wife Latife, who'd grown increasingly bitter during their brief, stormy marriage, Mustafa Kemal was in full control of the new Turkish republic.

At the beginning of July, 1928, Halide, Turhan and Nadji were among those summoned to a meeting at the presidential palace in Ankara, now the capital of Turkey. Early that morning, Turhan took

Halide to breakfast at the newly completed Tusan Hotel. Over tea, bread, olives, feta cheese and rose-petal jam, the traditional Turkish breakfast, Turhan remarked, "If anyone had told me a year ago that ten thousand houses would be crawling up Chankaya hill, I'd have thought him crazy. Now, Ankara spreads as far as the eye can see."

"Kemal's made so many changes, it's hard to keep up with him," she replied. "Three years ago, he outlawed the *fez* and decreed that every man must wear a hat when he went outdoors. European hat makers emptied their warehouses and sent every outdated Panama and Homburg they had to Anatolia. We snapped them up as if they were food and we'd not eaten in three days."

"The man has *sağlam tashak* – stone balls. I was with him the day he went to Kastamonu, our most reactionary province. The mountain folk didn't know what to expect. In one village, an artist had drawn a portrait of Kemal, the slayer of infidels, as a warrior with sweeping moustaches and a sword seven feet long! The president showed up clean-shaven, wearing a European summer suit, open-necked sport shirt, and Panama hat. Imagine the shock when the villagers saw the Gazi looking like an infidel!"

"I must say I approve of his position on women," Halide said.

"I don't know," Turhan replied, winking. "I'm not saying they should have to wear the veil in public, but giving them the vote is really too much!" She glared at him. Turhan playfully pulled out the blue "evil eye" pendant on the keychain he carried and held it toward her.

When they arrived at the presidential palace, they found a place next to Nadji and sat down. Promptly at the appointed hour, Mustafa Kemal strode in. His commanding blue eyes took in the audience.

"*Hosh geldiniz, arkadashlar!* Welcome my friends! Don't worry. This isn't the Grand National Assembly. No three hour speeches today.

I've called each of you here for a particular reason. Look around this room. Teachers, military officers, nurses, journalists. People who make a difference. Women as well as men. Not a politician in the lot." He waited for the laughter to subside before continuing. "The Turkish Republic is entering the twentieth century, nearly thirty years behind the rest of Europe."

He stopped and looked at his audience with pleasure. "There are as many women as men in Turkey. Progress is impossible when half our nation stays chained to the kitchen, the veil, and the home, while the other half reaches for the skies. That's why it's critically important that women as well as men build the new Turkey. For seven hundred years, we've turned our backs on the most basic element of our thought and communication, the Turkish language. We've absorbed Arabic writing and Persian literature. We speak every tongue but the Turkish our fathers brought here so long ago.

"This afternoon, I intend to announce to the Grand National Assembly that on December first, six months from now, we are returning to the Turkish language. Arabic writing and the Ottoman language will be abolished. Turkey will have a new alphabet based on Western European script. We'll start rebuilding our heritage from the ground up."

There was a collective gasp in the room.

"I will further announce the appointment of a commission for the purification of the language. Their goal will be to research literature – Turkish literature – from a thousand years ago, and find our heritage, the old words that have meaning. As new inventions come along, we may borrow foreign words, but the basic language will be our own.

"What does this have to do with each of you? Every man and woman in this room is young, healthy and vigorous. Each of you has been highly educated, some in European universities, others in Turkish schools. Each of you possesses qualities that have made you succeed beyond your peers. Most important, every one in this room is a human being of warmth, courage and determination, a person who influences others.

"Each of you can – and I hope each of you will – accept a special presidential posting. Anyone who does not feel he or she can make this sacrifice is free to turn my request down with no hard feelings and absolutely no recriminations. If you accept this challenge, the greatest in Turkey's history, the government will pay each of you reasonable, if not generous, compensation. We will guarantee that upon completion of your two years in the service of your country, those of you who are employed by others will be restored to your positions at no disadvantage."

Not one person who had attended the meeting refused the Gazi's challenge.

Each of the three friends had been assigned to work in Turkey's southeast quadrant. Halide was to go from village to village, teaching the new alphabet and language, then bringing the best and brightest from each place to Diyarbakır, where she would train them to become teachers.

Nadji was promoted to *binbashı,* Major, on detached duty from the Turkish General Staff, and assigned to Adana to supervise the education of all Turkish soldiers in his sector. Since the army regularly drew thousands of raw village recruits each year, there would be a large pool whose potential had never been tapped.

Turhan's task was to organize the creation and distribution of newspapers among the newly literate citizens of southeast Turkey.

2

The muezzin summoned the faithful to prayer, the first of five calls that would take place that day. Munir Hodja, the elderly village imam, went to the small, muddy stream that trickled through the outskirts of the village, a hundred feet from his house, and splashed some tepid, sour-smelling water onto his face and beard. The Prophet admonished complete cleanliness in all things. The Prophet had never lived in Suvarli.

The priest felt the knot in his stomach. He'd not moved his bowels in three days. His body felt plugged-up, stale. Thirty yards from the house, he squatted over the compost pile and tried again. Nothing. "*Bohk!*" he muttered, using the vulgar word for excrement. No, that wasn't the problem. *No bohk* was the problem, he thought bitterly. He'd tell the old woman later in the day. The one thing other than scolding, at which his wife was proficient, was knowing what medicinal vegetables and herbs loosened his bowels.

Munir bowed toward Mecca and intoned the words of the prayer by rote. Of a moment, he heard the voices of two young shepherds leading their sheep to pasture. Stupid imbeciles, he thought. What do they know of life? They laughed rudely and noisily, with not a care in the world. Wait 'til they were seventy-five, hunched over with arthritis, simply trying to make it from one day to the next with the minimum possible pain and stiffness. Wait 'til their hearing diminished so they could barely hear the whispers, "Smelly old goat. Father says not to say anything, just bow courteously, or he'll turn you into a worm." Wait 'til their teeth rotted away and all they could eat was thin gruel or oatmeal. Ah, youth! Why had he been robbed of a youth he'd never enjoyed?

When Munir was young, the caliph ensured that he enjoyed position and prestige in this pestilential village. Now the caliph was gone. The infidel held the reins of power. Four years ago, that Allah-cursed Mustafa Kemal had outlawed the *fez* and forced men to wear the *shapka*. The government banned the *mevlana*, the whirling dervishes in Konya. Abomination! Abominations all!

The imam picked listlessly at the lice in his hair and beard. Now, the worst thing of all! They'd declared the language of the Prophet illegal! Blasphemy! The "government" – he laughed bitterly to himself at this euphemism for the pack of Satan-lovers in Angora – was actually sending "teachers" to all parts of Anatolia to instruct peasants in the new alphabet. Heresy of heresies, there was even talk of publishing the Koran in the "Turkish" language. If they stayed in power long enough, Kemal and his bunch would bring about the collapse of Islam. The civilization Munir had worked so hard to preserve would die.

He'd heard that a so-called "teacher" was coming from Diyarbakır today. His spies had told him she was young, but grotesque looking, bent over. Good. If he could point out her devil-created shortcomings, so much the better. She was a woman, little more than a vessel into which you poured your seed, hoping to bring forth sons to carry on your name. You couldn't trust a woman. What a shame the Anatolians had never adopted the Arabic custom of clipping a girl's clitoris early in her life. That way she'd never be led into debauchery by her accursed sensuality. Munir felt bitter glee as he contemplated the scorn he'd heap on this ugly female. Another thought dampened his ardor. Don't underestimate the enemy. Satan appears in different forms. Not to be on guard would be foolish indeed. And Munir was not a fool.

"Are you certain you don't want protection, Halide? Suvarli's the heart of Muslim reactionary resistance. They still stone people. It would be days before we could reach you."

"No, thank you, Nadji. If I force learning on these people from the barrel of a gun, it will soon be rejected. It was good of you to accompany me as far as Pazarjık." As their car pulled into the town square, Halide saw a man of indeterminate middle age waving at them.

"I see my host is waiting." As they pulled up beside a well-used buckboard, she said, "*Günaydin,* good morning, Muhtar Effendim, peace be with you," she said, using both his title, *Muhtar* – village headman – and the honorific *Effendim*, which had recently replaced the Ottoman *Effendi*. "Many, many thanks for your courtesy in coming for me."

"*Hosh geldiniz*, Halide Hanım, Major Akdemir," the man replied. "Please call me Yakup. I'm sorry our village doesn't have a motorcar nor even a tractor, but it's my privilege to offer you what poor transport we have."

"Yakup Effendim," Halide said, "I'm proud and happy to ride with you, provided I can ride on the seat. Some years ago, when I first arrived in Turkey, I traveled an entire night hidden beneath hay and manure in a farm wagon. What you offer is far superior!"

"Have you no more baggage than that?" he asked, looking at her single grip.

"Only a small box of simple books, which Major Akdemir will load on my behalf. Most Anatolians don't acquire this much in a lifetime. How can I hope to gain the confidence of Suvarli's villagers if I parade myself in finery that surpasses theirs?"

"But you have so little."

"What I carry is in my head and in my heart. Allah will provide the rest."

"Very unlikely you'll be able to depend on Allah, at least as He's perceived in Suvarli. Our *imam* decreed you're to be shunned."

"I'm not surprised. I've heard Munir *Hodja* is not pleased at my arrival."

"An understatement, Hanım. If he had his way, you'd be stoned as you entered the village."

"We'll have to see what we can do about that," she said, simply. She thanked Nadji once again and climbed onto the seat next to the *muhtar*. As they headed north, Halide sensed the vast loneliness of this barren land. Dried hills with little life. Dusty, often muddy, cart tracks, which could never be negotiated by an automobile. Except the man sitting beside her, not another living soul as far as the eye could see.

They approached the village, a small group of mud huts gathered about a rounded hill, at sunset. Weed-covered paths radiating from the village center served as streets. "There are three hundred people in Suvarli," the *muhtar* said. "No electricity, no piped water, no gas, no firewood. Each family saves sheep dung all year and burns it for warmth during the winter. Our standards are primitive, but we survive." They came to a low, stone building. Outside, a Turkish flag hung limply from a wooden pole. "My home and the village meeting house," he said. "There's an extra room for guests. It's yours for as long as you're here. There is no toilet in the house. There's a shed out back. Most villagers use the open area behind their homes."

Next morning, Halide was just finishing breakfast when she heard the muffled noise of a crowd gathering outside the muhtar's home. There was a sharp pounding on the front door. "Yakup bey, open up! We hear you've a new visitor. We'd like to extend a proper greeting."

"Fikret, the *imam's* nasty errand boy," Yakup said. "I can just imagine the nature of his 'proper' greeting. He's been waiting twenty years for the old man to die so he might become *imam*. Meanwhile, he toadies up to Munir as if he were the favorite son."

The *muhtar* went to the door. "Peace be with you, Fikret Effendi," he said politely. "We're pleased you honor our unworthy home with your presence. Might we beg, in Allah's name, your indulgence in allowing us to finish our meager morning meal?"

"Oh, *Muhtar*," Fikret replied, his voice making the honorific sound like an insult, "we're so sorry to have distressed you so early in the day. Perhaps because we've been at prayer since dawn the day somehow seems much longer. Ah, I see your guest has risen from the table," he said, as Halide came to the door. "Good morning to you, Hanım Effendi," he said, bowing low. As he did so, he passed wind noisily. The men behind him burst into raucous laughter.

"Why Fikret bey," Halide said, as unruffled as though she were a stone, "I'd not expected to be greeted with music as well as words." There was sharp laughter of a different kind, this time directed against the imam's assistant. He glared angrily about. All fell silent as a tall, grim-looking old man with unkempt beard approached the door stiffly.

"Allah is great, *Muhtar*," he said. "I see you submitted to the pack of infidels in Angora and housed their harlot. Caution! If you go to bed with dogs, you wake up with fleas."

"Well said, *hodja*," Yakup retorted. "By the way, are you still having problems with lice in your beard?" There was an audible gasp from the assembly. They knew there was no love lost between the priest and the headman, but such a riposte was unseemly, deliberately meant to fuel the fires of anger.

"Gentlemen, gentlemen," Halide interjected. "The Prophet says, 'Let not the sun of day be blotted by the storm clouds of anger.' Welcome, Hodja Effendi. It was good of you to come greet me."

"*Greet* you?" the old man sneered. "Welcome the devil to my home? Not in my lifetime, woman. I came to see if you were as ugly as they said. Indeed you are. Satan has given up trying to lure mankind with comeliness. He is now revealed for what he is."

"*I* see, Hodja Effendi, that you seem to have forgotten the admonition 'Extend kindness to the stranger in your house'" she replied. "Aren't you supposed to teach the Prophet's ways by word and deed?"

"Government harlot!" the priest spat contemptuously. "Don't tell me what the Prophet says. I know exactly how a guest is to be treated. Hospitality does not extend to the devil's agent. Such a one is to be cast out with evil spirits and excrement!"

By now, word had spread throughout the village of the confrontation. The meeting created more excitement than the villagers had seen in several years. Halide walked onto the porch. More than a hundred men crowded the area immediately around the flag pole. Women stayed discreetly in the background, their faces partially hidden by coarse cloth veils. The *imam* seized the opportunity. "My villagers, look upon the ugliness the devil sets before you with the aid of the thieves and cutthroats in Angora! Would Allah have sanctioned the creation of such a deformed monstrosity? Had this girl been born in Suvarli, would she have been allowed to live? Of course not. She'd have been carrion for the wolves. Allah cast the mark of Satan upon her with his own hand. From someone so grotesque and misshapen, one can only hear lies. Let us throw her out of the village now. Now! Now! Now!" he exhorted, his voice rising.

Several of the hodja's followers took up the chant, but not everyone in the crowd was moved. Many owed allegiance to the *muhtar*. Most, who had no feelings one way or the other, felt embarrassed at the *imam*'s want of good manners. As he sensed this, the hodja changed his approach, raising his arms to calm the crowd. "My children," he said, in a conciliatory tone. "Do not think I disobey the Word of the Prophet. As one who has brought that Word to you, who has interpreted the Word for you these many years, I would defer, even give this devil her due. Perhaps she might grace us with her 'wisdom.'" There was snickering in the crowd. "Halide Hanım," he nodded in her direction. "Please address us simple, backward villagers. Speak as my guest, if you will."

Halide controlled her anger. If she were to rise to the old man's bait, she'd only fall into his trap. She came forward, dwarfed by his size, repulsed by the sour odor that emanated from him.

"*Günaydin*, villagers of Suvarli," she began. Her voice was soft. The crowd moved closer to hear her better. "I thank you all, the *imam* included, for allowing me the honor to come to your village and spread what little knowledge I can. The *imam* told you I am ugly and misshapen. That is true," she said. There was a gasp from the crowd. "But he is mistaken when he implies that nothing good can come from the lips of someone less attractive than he." For the first time that morning the hodja felt the sting of derisive laughter.

"Once there was a king who'd stored his fine yogurt in earthenware containers from time out of mind. One day, his vizier told him it was unseemly for a ruler of his stature to store such precious stuff in plain vessels. It would be far more appropriate to use gold amphoras. The king did as he advised and threw out the ugly clay pottery. Seven-times-seven days later, he held a great banquet. He invited kings, princes and nobles from all corners of the earth. When he attempted to serve the yogurt, he found it tasted sour and metallic. He hauled the cellar master before him and bellowed angrily, 'You have but one minute to tell me why I should not have you beheaded forthwith for shaming the greatest celebration in the history of my kingdom!' The old servant, who knew that death would come when Allah decreed, said, 'Your majesty, everything the All-Wise put on earth serves its own purpose. Even the sultan of sultans cannot change the laws of nature. Yogurt and gold do not mix. If you try to force marriage between them, only enmity will result. No matter how ugly the earthenware vessel, it serves as the best protection for the yogurt's delicate flavor.' The servant was spared and the sultan humbled. From that time forward, the king stored his yogurt as he had in the past, and thereafter he lived a long and happy life, honoring 'til his dying day the plain, clay amphoras which so well nurtured his precious treasure.

"I am as plain and ugly as the meanest earthenware vessel. But I am filled with knowledge that may help you better your own lives. What have you got to lose by tasting what I have to offer? Judge for yourselves whether or not what I bring is sour and metallic, or sweet and worthy."

The *imam* was beside himself with rage. How could he possibly have walked into this she-devil's trap? Yet that is just what he'd done. He rudely pushed in front of her and said, "My people, the Evil One's serpent spins stories of gossamer to lure you into her web of lies! For more than fifty years, I, and I alone, have brought you the Prophet's Holy Word."

"Is that so, Hodja Effendi?" Halide said, in a voice sharp enough to be heard above his oration. "If you are so steeped in learning, why haven't you set up schools so your people can read the Prophet's Word for themselves?"

"Silence!" he shouted "How dare you, a lowly woman, a stranger, tell me, the *imam*, what our people want and need? How *dare* you say you bring the Prophet's Word to our people, when the very devils who sent you decreed we can no longer read the Koran in His own tongue?"

"How dare *you*," Halide said with equal force, "deprive men and women of the right to read the Prophet's Words in language they can understand, and interpret for themselves what those words mean?"

"My people don't need book knowledge. They have the wisdom of a thousand years. They use that wisdom to survive. Allah placed me on earth to succor their spiritual needs, to guide them through difficult times."

"And just who told you that Allah placed you here for that purpose? Did the Lord come waving a great wand and say, 'Munir, I, Allah, appoint you to interpret the Koran to the village of Suvarli?'" She hesitated for an instant as she saw the villagers' frightened looks. She realized she'd challenged the unchallengeable, and undoubtedly had gone too far by insulting one of their own. The crowd started to turn away.

"Good villagers," she said. "I apologize publicly to your honorable *imam* if my words have offended him. I do not mean to insult him. But I believe with all my heart that knowledge will open the door to a better life for all of you." She stepped off the porch and into the midst of the crowd. She gave them time to realize no earthquake was going to knock them from their feet. The sun remained shining as before. "My friends," she continued, "Many of you believe what I said was an affront to the All Merciful. Yet, here we stand, you and I, unharmed. The day is beautiful, the gentle breeze pleasant. What a wonderful day for a new beginning, one that would make Allah Himself smile down with approval. There is so much I want to learn from you – how to weave, how to sew, how to plant and how to reap. I have much to share with you as well. When you learn to read, you will unlock the Koran's secrets and bring them into your own souls. You'll find out what goes on in the world beyond Suvarli, even beyond Marash and Gaziantep. You can take control of your own destiny. You need not be held prisoner by the old ways. Many things must not be abandoned, but others can – and should – be improved upon. Let's begin a wonderful adventure together, you and I. Let us be friends."

By cockcrow next morning, Halide was fully dressed. "Do you think I was too forward yesterday, Yakup Effendim?" she asked her host at breakfast.

"It's hard for me to say, Halide. This is a very traditional village. Our ways have been established for a long, long time."

"And yet, you welcomed me into your home, knowing who I was and what I was about. Why, Yakup?"

The *muhtar* put his glass on the wooden table and cupped his chin in his left palm for a few moments before he answered. Halide gazed steadily at the man. He dressed no differently from his neighbors. Black pants, white shirt, dark cap. His calloused hands gave evidence of a lifetime of hard work. He could have been anywhere from forty years of age to past sixty. There was something special about him. Something that had motivated the villagers to elevate him to headman. He drummed his left index finger against his cheek, seemingly lost in thought. When he finally answered, he spoke in slow cadence, without hesitation. "As I said, ours is a very traditional village. Hospitality to the stranger is the most sacred of our customs, as it is throughout the Muslim world."

"I appreciate that, but you knew you were hosting an agent of change – and I sense much of that change is unwelcome."

"True, Halide."

"So why put yourself at risk?"

"Because some things must change. Many years ago, I learned to read – not well, but enough for my purposes – at the government school. Sometimes – not often, for this is not a wealthy village – an outsider happens by. Someone's relative, a trader far from the normal routes, a cast-off from another village. He spends a night, perhaps two, in my home. After all, where else would he stay in this village? We talk. Occasionally – very occasionally – he will leave some memento behind. A book, perhaps, or a month-old news journal he believes is good for nothing more than wrapping food.

"When that happens, I find some way to hide the journal. Allah has graced me with regular movements, and each morning when I go to the out-building I take a portion of the paper with me. I read very slowly. Sometimes I spell out the word sounds. I learn slowly, but I learn. By the time I've read the paper a few times, the better part of a year has gone by. I see pictures of motor cars. I read there are new machines that can do as much work in an hour as ten men perform in a day. I think, 'With machines such as these, we needn't permanently bow our backs bending in the field. Things would be easier for my people.' I start to believe that maybe all change is not bad.

"I see our best boys grow up and move from the village. They say they're looking for a better life. Do they find it? I don't know. But I do know that our village shrinks a little each year, and these fine young men aren't replaced."

"Then, Yakup Effendim, you don't see what I'm doing as a further threat to the survival of the village?"

"No," the *muhtar* said thoughtfully. "I don't. You see, one carries his character on his back wherever he goes, just like a turtle. Our young people flee to the cities and towns because there's no future for them in the village. Many become disappointed, but by then there's no return for them, since they'd only be coming back to boredom and the old ways they fled from in the first place. If, somehow, they see they can gain satisfaction within their own village, that their lives make a difference here, perhaps a few more will stay. It is only by openness to the ideas of the young that we have a chance to keep them in the village."

"And you see my teaching as accomplishing that?"

The *muhtar* smiled. "I didn't say that, Hanım Effendi. I said, 'It is only by opening our minds to the ideas of our young people that we may hope to keep them in the village.' One must try many ideas and see which ones work."

"I'll know within the hour whether this one will work," Halide said. "Do you think it was a good idea to schedule the meeting for outdoors? It looks like it will be a lovely day. Most work in the fields should be done by noon."

"One would hope. I think you may have offended their sensibilities by inviting women as well as men to the lessons. Such a thing would have been unthinkable in the old days."

"There's only one way to tell. Wish me luck, Yakup Bey."

"I do, Hanım Effendim. I fear you'll need it."

Shortly after midmorning, Halide walked to a small, square field, a few hundred yards from the *muhtar's* house. Earlier, she'd cleared a level area of ground and found small sticks, so that anyone who wanted to do so could write letters in the clean earth. Yakup had constructed a rectangular wooden board for her, and had set up several benches around the board. Halide attached several sheets of white paper to the board, and put some books and writing implements on the ground beside her.

She did not expect an overwhelming turnout. Perhaps ten percent of the population, thirty people, would appear for the first lesson, if only for curiosity. Her disappointment grew with each step she took. There were two people sitting on the benches, a young woman in her early twenties, and an old man who might have been anywhere between seventy and the grave. Halide went up to the board.

"Good morning," she began. "My name is Halide. We're here today to begin a new adventure. Although I expected more people, I'm thankful you two are here. What's your name, Baba Effendi?" she asked, using the honorific for father as courtesy demanded.

"Ehh?" he asked.

"I said, '*What's your name, Baba Effendi?*'"

"I'm sorry, Hanım. I'm mostly deaf. Come right up to grandpa. Don't be afraid." Halide saw out of the corner of her eye that the young woman was suppressing laughter.

When Halide was close enough to be heard clearly, she shouted in the old man's ear, "*What's your name, Baba Effendi?*"

"Nasrullah."

"Do you know why you're here, Nasrullah?"

"Of course. Because Allah placed a bench here and I'm tired. Why are *you* here, Hanım?"

The young woman could no longer stifle her laughter. Halide kept her composure. "I'm here to teach you a new language."

"Why, Hanım? I've survived seventy-four summers. The old language suits me just fine, thank you."

"Will you stay and listen to what I have to say?"

"It doesn't matter to me. I can't hear you anyway."

"Very well, Nasrullah Effendi. Let me show you something." She walked over to where she'd placed a pile of sticks. She wrote the name

Nasrullah in the dirt by his feet. "Can you draw the same thing I did, Effendi?"

"I can't see very well, but I'll try." Stiffly, slowly, imprecisely, Nasrullah drew in the earth with his stick. The resemblance to what Halide had drawn was slight.

"Nasrullah Effendi, please may I help you?"

"You may, daughter."

She guided the man's hand. The result was much better. They tried two more times. Then Halide said, "Now try it yourself." He did. This time there was a definite resemblance to what Halide had drawn.

"Are you able to write, baba?"

"No. No one in the village except the imam and the muhtar can read or write."

"And now there's you, Nasrullah. The marks you've made in the dirt spell your name."

The man looked incredulous.

"On Allah's mercy, it's true, Baba." She turned to the young woman. "What is your name, Hanım Effendi?"

"I am not a hanım effendi, an honored woman. I am Sezer the orphan." She had an alert, intelligent look, and was quite pretty in spite of the mean clothing she wore.

"Sezer, you may not be *hanım effendi* in your eyes, but you are in mine. Everyone is equal in the eyes of Allah, man or woman, young or old, rich or poor. We all suffer from the same disease. We are human beings. Why did you come?"

"I want to leave this village, Halide Hanım. Yesterday, you said learning was the way to escape the chains that bind us. I want to do that."

"Very well. Let's begin by writing your name in the earth."

The next day, five people attended lessons. Nasrullah brought two more old men, to show them he'd learned to write his name. They were eager to prove they could do the same thing. As soon as they'd learned to do so, the three of them wandered off, quite proud of their accomplishment. That left Sezer and a young man of sixteen, Yurtash, who apologized to Halide for not having come the previous day. He told her he'd worked in the fields with his father until sundown, gathering in the last of the harvest.

By week's end, Halide's class had swelled to ten, less than she'd hoped for, but a start. She knew the earliest lessons would be frustrating, and that if any of her students were discouraged they would not return. She gave individual attention and assistance to everyone who attended, no matter what the hour. She used simple language and whatever materials were available. A month after Halide arrived, she had thirty students, a tenth of the population.

"It started slowly, Yakup Bey," Halide remarked one evening. "But I think the people really want to learn, after all."

"It looks that way," the *muhtar* said. "You must remember though, the villagers are like children with a new toy. It's easy for them to write their names in the earth with sticks. It's something else to learn to read and write."

"That will come, Effendim."

"For a few of them, yes. But these people work in the fields or sit in the chay house and gossip all day. They're not inclined to do anything more than they must to stay alive. You're asking them to change a lifetime of habits, and you add insult to injury by asking them to do extra work to bring about that change. Soon they may tire of the toy."

At first the *imam* refused to acknowledge Halide's presence. When word leaked out to him that her efforts were apparently successful, he employed more active means of fighting her. One morning she opened the front door and found a large pile of fresh dung barring her exit. Another day she found huge holes dug in her writing field, with hay and manure tamped into the depressions. One of the hodja's followers was always in the immediate area to note her reaction. Invariably, she simply stepped around the feces, or patiently created a new field in which her students could write. The day's lesson was delayed a couple hours at most.

A few days later, the hodja walked to the village outskirts, where she was conducting class, and glared balefully at her. Next day, he appeared again, but said nothing. That night, when she returned to her room, she found blood splattered over the walls and floors. The following day, she continued teaching as though nothing had happened. The old man was there again, an evil smirk on his face. Halide smiled in his direction, but otherwise did not acknowledge his existence.

By the end of the second month, it looked as if the *muhtar's* dire prediction was coming true. Half the students had stopped coming to her classes altogether. Of the fifteen remaining, a third showed unmistakable signs of boredom. Sezer and Yurtash still came each day. Their progress was by far the most promising. Halide consoled herself that even if only five learned to read and write, that would be a beginning.

But more crushing news followed. Yurtash did not come to lessons for three days. On the fourth day, he came late in the afternoon. His eyes were red, as though he'd been crying. He waited until Halide was alone, then approached her. "What is it, Yurtash?" Halide asked. "Is something wrong?"

"Hanım Effendi, I must stop lessons. I cannot come any more."

"What?" She was stunned. "But you're doing so well, Yurtash. You could become a natural teacher."

"I'm sorry," he said. "My father says the new ways are not good and they'll lead our people away from the true path."

"But Yurtash, you know better. You've been here every day. Do you fear what you're learning?"

"My father tells me I'm too young to know what's good for me. He says I've become lazy since I started school and that I don't work well during the day because I'm too tired from studying at night."

"That's not so, is it?"

"I can't say, Hanım Effendi. He's my father. I have no choice but to obey him. Thank you for trying to open the gate for me. Perhaps some day in the future..." He bowed his head and walked quickly away.

That night, Halide cried herself to sleep. She remained in her room next day. When she returned to her field the following morning, she was surprised to find twenty children between the ages of five and ten in attendance. She soon learned the reason for this. The *muhtar* and his wife had used their influence to exhort every young mother in the village to send their child to lessons. They had used a wonderful combination of guilt and envy, asking the women how they would bear the shame of being rude to a guest, then asking them how they would feel if there child was the only one in the village who hadn't learned how to read and write.

Time passed swiftly. All too soon it was time for Halide to leave Suvarli and return to Diyarbakır. She'd experienced the sobering frustration of trying to overturn age-old traditions. Of three hundred villagers who'd been illiterate when she'd come to Suvarli, only Sezer could read the government primers. Another eight, mostly children, could follow simple words with their fingers. Twenty more could read and write their names, but that was the extent of their literacy. She'd brought the joy of reading to less than three percent of the population. At that rate, it would take the Gazi a hundred years to achieve his goals. She felt dismal.

Nonetheless, courtesy demanded she attend the village celebration to bid her farewell that evening. The men slaughtered five sheep. On the afternoon before the festivities, Halide learned from the *muhtar's* wife how to make shepherd's salad.

"It's easy. For each few persons, you take a small onion, a few tomatoes, a green pepper or two, a cucumber and a handful of parsley. Chop them up. Sprinkle some sugar and squeeze lemon juice over the whole thing, mix it together and there it is. Since time beyond reckoning, shepherds have taken it with them to the fields. When you taste some, you'll see why."

Just before they left to go to the feast, Halide asked the headman, "Yakup Effendim, where did I go wrong? Why did I fail in Suvarli?"

"I don't believe you failed at all, Halide Hanim. Only your expectations may have been a little bit too high. Our villagers don't take quickly to change. I'm not a man of the world, but I think most people don't accept a major change in their lives easily. When a man or woman gets used to wearing a shirt or a veil, these things become comfortable. People hesitate to part with them. It's the same with anything new. Take the *imam*. Despite what you may think, he's not a bad man, but he's an unhappy one. It's no secret that he and his wife are hardly even friends. Yet they've stayed together and fought one another for more than fifty years. If one of them dies, the other won't be far behind, if only to make sure heaven is not *that* perfect for the other. Picture life as a large circle. Men and women go around within that circle, but they rarely leave it. Perhaps you asked too many to depart that circle, too soon."

"Kemal asked me to help bring Turkey into the modern century so it can take its place among the advanced nations of the world."

"That's fine for Kemal and for Ankara. Things don't move so fast in Suvarli. Blood does not move from the heart to the toes in an instant. Change takes time. It won't come at all if you push people out of their accustomed circle. Rather, let them enlarge their circle slowly. Then change will come."

"I was so certain they wanted to learn."

"Halide, it is the province of the young to transform the world and to try to move heaven and earth to force older folk to accept the new order. When it doesn't work as quickly as they want, they feel they've failed. That's not so. One out of every ten people in the village is better off because you came here. How many people would that be in a city the size of Istanbul?"

Halide smiled for the first time in days. "Thank you for your wisdom, Muhtar Effendim. It seems I can learn from the old ways as well."

Halide's mood lifted. She thought about the villagers who'd helped her get to Metin years ago in Chandarla. They were no different from those in Suvarli. While they might not accept what the outlander had to say, it never diminished their courtesy. They would move into the future much more slowly than the government – or she – would have wished. But sooner or later, they would move forward at their own pace. She uttered a small prayer, "Allah, don't ever let them part with the values they possess. Don't let them be ruined. Don't let them be trampled by those who consider themselves more progressive. Grant them peace."

Just before dawn next morning, Halide heard a soft, rasping noise outside her window. She opened the latch. "Sezer? What are you doing up at this hour?"

"I'm going with you, Hanım Effendim."

"But you've got a home here in the village."

"No, Halide Hanım, I don't. I'm an orphan. I've no dowry. No man will marry me. There's nothing to hold me here."

"Aren't you frightened? It's a whole new life."

"That's just why I want to go with you. I want to become a teacher like you, so I can give others the gift you've given me. Then, perhaps, *two* more teachers will come from the next village. People won't change overnight, but someday they'll see that books open many doors. Then they'll want to learn. When that day arrives, our country will need many more teachers than we have. Let me be among the first, Halide Hanım."

Halide smiled. Wasn't this exactly why she'd come to these villages, to find the teachers who would one day bring Anatolia into the twentieth century? This intelligent, attractive young woman was eager, dedicated, everything the Gazi had told her to look for. "Sezer Hanım," she said. "If that's what you want, you are truly the hero I knew you'd be. Have you any things to take?"

"My clothes, my mind and my heart."

"In that case, what are we waiting for? We've got centuries of work to do in a very few years. Two can bear that load better than one. Hanım Effendim – and indeed you deserve that title, Sezer – bring your heart, your mind, and your clothes. Let's get an early start. You and I are going to help change the face of Anatolia!"

3

Within a week after he went to Diyarbakır, Turhan stopped in the village where he'd been born. He was disappointed to find that his grandmother had died. In the Muslim tradition, she was buried next to Grandfather, in a small cemetery at the edge of the village. Turhan visited their graves and bowed his head. "Baba, I've returned for a little while. I did what you said. I learned to read and write. You were right, Grandpa. Education unlocked many doors for me. So much has happened in this land. Many changes you fought for have come to pass. There's a new law that everyone is equal to everyone else. Armenians, Greeks, Jews, Turks, it doesn't matter. We live in a new Turkey, Baba. I think you'd like the changes. You'd be proud to know I'm helping to bring them about. I don't know when I'll come this way again, Grandpa. I needed to tell you these things, even if, wherever you are, you can see them yourself. Thank you, Grandfather, for everything. I love you." Turhan knelt to where he felt Grandfather's heart would be and kissed the earth. Then he went to a nearby field, where the last of the year's wildflowers were growing. He picked a handful and placed them where he thought Grandpa's feet would be. He had closed the circle.

The following week, he searched out Jalal the butcher. He was delighted to find that Jalal was not only very much among the living, but in the same robust health as when Turhan had last seen him twenty years ago. Now seventy-one, he'd retired five years ago, and was one of Diyarbakır's wealthier citizens. His elegant mansion did little to conceal that Jalal had remained the practical, down-to-earth, happy man he'd been when Turhan was twelve. "How in the world did you manage to find me? For all you know, I'd have been long dead by now."

"Blind luck, Jalal Effendim." Turhan smiled. The retired butcher, as beefy as ever, looked no closer to the grave than he had the day Turhan had told him he was leaving on the caravan with Ibrahim. "I've become involved with Kemal's government."

"So I'd heard, little stripling," Jalal said. "I'd wondered when the world famous Turhan Türkoğlu would finally come to see an old friend."

Turhan blushed, embarrassed. "I did try to contact you in..."

"Nineteen eighteen. Ten years ago, lad. Never mind excuses. I've followed your emerging career with great interest, and I must say, with great pride. You'll have dinner with us, of course?" Jalal asked.

"By all means. But would you allow me to *purchase* a lamb loin for you, Effendim?"

The old man doubled over with laughter. "So you remembered, my little thief," he said, grabbing Turhan around the waist and hugging him. "Cheyhan," he called, "come see our third son, the prodigal returned at last!" The woman who trundled out was an even larger version of the burly butcher, with a smile as oversized as the rest of her. Turhan recognized her as a somewhat older, substantially better-fed version of the woman who'd occupied the egg stall three down from Jalal's. Turhan felt like a boy again.

Over dinner that night, Turhan recalled the happy memories of his life with Jalal. How quickly bad times had been forgotten. The butcher and his wife were eager to hear of Turhan's adventures since he'd left Diyarbakır seventeen years ago. After their meal, the old man took Turhan into his capacious library, where talk became more intimate and confidential. "Gönül's fine, fat, and living in Iskenderun," Jalal began. Turhan blushed. "No need to feel embarrassed," he continued. "Did you think I didn't know about you two?"

"But Ertuğrul?"

"He's probably the only one who never knew about it, may his soul rest in peace. She made a good second marriage with a man far nearer her own age. She telephones occasionally and visits once every couple of years."

"What about Alkimi?"

"She died eight years ago. Rumor has it she was over a hundred years old. I'm over seventy and she was an old woman when I first met her. In a way, it's a good thing she passed on before things had changed too much. Each year the caravans were becoming fewer and fewer. It was the only life she'd ever known and when the Angel came to claim her, she was right where she'd always wanted to be."

Another circle closed.

"What about you, sprout?" Jalal asked genially. "I'd have thought you'd have a wife and three or four sons by now. You're more than thirty years old, aren't you?"

"Thirty-two. I've been much too busy to find the right woman."

"Nonsense, Turhan. You're out in the villages. You meet people from all over this country. Granted, you probably wouldn't feel comfortable with a high-born lady from Istanbul, but there are millions of good, strong village girls who'd give anything to make you a perfect life's companion. You should go out and find one."

"It's not nearly so easy as you make it sound, Jalal Effendim." Turhan shifted uncomfortably in his chair.

"Nonsense! I've had the happiest of lives because I've shared it with more than one good woman. Mark my words, boy, without a female to balance things out, all the success in the world is meaningless. What about the friend you mentioned, Halide?"

"The thought never crossed my mind. In her heart, she's had two lovers, one who died at Gelibolu and one, Turkey, that's struggling to stay alive in the Twentieth Century. Besides, she's a graduate of the Sorbonne, a Parisienne..."

"And someone you could never hope to aspire to?" The butcher looked at Turhan without blinking. "You'll pardon me if I sound brutally direct, but I've always been honest with you. There's an old saying, 'You can take the boy out of the country, but you can't take the country out of the boy.' Are you saying you'd be afraid to compete with Halide in a day-to-day relationship?"

"Perhaps, Effendim." Why had Jalal always been able to touch the raw nerves beneath the surface? "I don't know. We're such good friends, and we've been through so much together. I could never think of her as a lover. I'm certain she feels the same way."

"Not to worry. I'm sure when the time is right, you'll find someone." Jalal, sensing Turhan's discomfort, moved on to another subject. "Tell me all about this grand program you and our esteemed *Gazi* are bringing to Turkey."

Turhan, relieved at being spared Jalal's deeper exploration of feelings he didn't want to contend with, spent the next hour telling his host of Mustafa Kemal's plans to modernize Anatolia and to spread knowledge from frontier to frontier. "In fact, Effendim, I need your advice. I've received a request to travel far to the east, to a place so small it exists on none but the largest maps of Turkey. It's certainly not something I've done in the past, but..."

East of Lake Van, the land was wild and starkly beautiful. For the past four days, Turhan had not lost sight of *Ağrı Dağ*, Turkey's highest peak. He'd read that the ancients had called it Mount Ararat. There were few farms. Villages were more than fifty miles apart. From Van to the Iranian frontier, the government post road turned from macadam to gravel, then to rutted dirt. This land of goats and sheep, high grass and horsemen, went on for countless miles. A few thousand Turks shared the land with a dozen other peoples. Turkey's eastern borders were indefinite. The government maintained military garrisons at Kars in the north and Hakkarı in the south. There was a landing strip at each place. It took only a day to fly the five hundred miles between these outposts. To a surface traveler, these provincial forts may as well have been separated by oceans.

The April sun had not melted the snow, which still blanketed the highlands. Turhan's destination was the village of Dorutay, perhaps twenty-five miles from the border. The operative word was *"perhaps,"* for the muddy path built by the government ended at the village. Not even dirt tracks stretched beyond.

News of the dramatic events reshaping Anatolia had spread to these highlands. Six months ago, the village had sent a delegation to Van entreating the regional administrator to send a teacher. Turhan heard of the group's five day pilgrimage while he was in Diyarbakır. Moved by the remarkable strength of character it had taken for these proud people to ask for help, he determined to go to the frontier village himself. "We should be there in another hour," the *muhtar* said.

Despite the noonday sun and the heavy, fleece-lined coat he'd borrowed in Van, Turhan shivered as icy wind whipped down off the mountains ahead. It had been years since he'd ridden a horse. Only today had the saddle sores begun to abate. The compact bay gelding reminded him of another steed he'd ridden so long ago. What ever happened to *Yildiz*, he wondered? He'd given the little mare to Zari Ben David as a parting gift, just before he left for Istanbul. She'd been overwhelmed, and had hugged him ecstatically. What ever happened to Zari? He felt guilty for not having stayed in touch.

Before they came in sight of the village, Turhan heard excited shouting that seemed to move from left to right, and back again. As they breasted a rise, Turhan saw a large, flat, snow covered field in the midst of several hills. A hundred men stood at the edge of the field, cheering noisily as two teams of five horsemen each rode their small ponies toward and away from one another. The horses made impossibly tight turns, their tails bobbed, their manes flowing. Occasionally, one of the horsemen let fly with a long, thin, wooden lance. While Turhan watched, one rider hit another with an accurate throw of his javelin, and a thunderous cheer broke out among the onlookers.

"*Jirit*," the head man remarked. "The favorite winter sport in eastern Anatolia for nine hundred years. Warriors brought it when they came west from Mangalistan, beyond the Indus River. This will be the last game this year. Our growing season starts in a fortnight. There are ten horsemen on each team. Riders throw wooden sticks at one another. Each hit is worth one point. The game lasts several hours. Every time a pole is thrown, a rider must return to his own side for another. That's why you hardly ever see an entire team attack at one time."

"No one is wearing a protective helmet of any kind. Can't they get hurt pretty badly?"

"Oh, yes. Four or five players are seriously injured each year. As soon as they heal, they're in the saddle again, clamoring for more.

Bravo, Ahmet!" the headman called out, as a rider and his white horse whirled one-hundred-eighty degrees and the horseman let fly his lance in a single fluid motion. "My son," the muhtar said, proudly. "The skill is not so much in throwing the rod, but in maneuvering the horse."

"One day, I'd like to try my hand at *jirit*," Turhan said.

"Help this village learn to read and write, and I promise we'll teach you."

"That's a bargain," said Turhan.

During the next months, Turhan succeeded beyond his most optimistic expectations. The hardy villagers thirsted for knowledge. Unlike their suppressed sisters farther to the west, Dorutay's women eagerly attended lessons alongside their menfolk. Turhan taught from sunup to sundown. The villagers worked in shifts, so Turhan was surrounded by at least ten students every waking hour of his day. At the end of two months, thirty-five out of a population of two hundred could read and write simple, direct sentences. Ten were already reading primers.

"What do you do in Ankara, Effendim?" the headman asked one day.

"I'm a newspaper writer."

"What is a news-paper?"

"Just what it sounds like. We write about whatever's interesting. Sometimes it may be news about a village. Other times, we may want to know what's going on in the rest of Turkey, even the rest of the world. Once we decide what we want to write, we print the same words on different sheets of paper so that many people can read what is going on."

"How can you print so many copies?"

"The old fashioned way is to write several pieces of paper by hand."

"*Vakh*! We're just learning to write. It would take us a hundred days to write out ten newspapers. By that time, the news would be so old no one would be interested."

"There are other ways. Is there a typewriter in Dorutay?"

"One," the *muhtar* replied. "But it's old and rusted. No one ever uses it."

"How do you communicate with other towns?"

"Whenever a scribe happens by, he writes letters by hand. It would take a scribe forever to write out these news-papers you talk about. Is there no easier way?"

"Yes, *Muhtar* Bey, there is. In big cities, and even in some of the larger towns, they have presses that can print the same thing hundreds of times in an hour. In Diyarbakır, they print thousands of news-papers every day."

"*Yasik*! What a shame we have no funds to purchase such a machine. This news-paper you talk about sounds almost like a letter addressed to the whole world from Dorutay."

"I never thought of it that way, but it's even more than that. It's a letter to *and from* the whole world to one another. It lets people know what others are doing. Suppose Ozalp and Saray," he said, mentioning two neighboring villages, "have games of *jirit* where a team from one village competes against a team from another. Not everyone can travel from Dorutay to Saray, but if there's a news-paper distributed to the people, the results of the match are known in all three villages."

"*Vakh*!" the muhtar growled. "We don't need a news-paper for that. There's nothing in these hills we don't know about within a few hours after it's happened."

"That was not such a good example, Effendim, but surely you could think of a use for such a journal?"

The *muhtar* thought for a moment. Then his eyes brightened, "Suppose there's a comely girl from Erchek whose father wants to marry her off. He could print an article in the paper and the news might spread to many villages. We could charge the man a few *kurush* to print the article since he would benefit. With enough paid articles, we could pay for what it costs to print the paper. If we ask readers to pay money to buy the paper, one day we could even buy a printing press."

"*Muhtar* Effendim, you have the heart of a businessman and the mind of an editor!"

Six men, the *muhtar* among them, became very excited about the news-paper project. To prepare for the journal, which would one day come into being, news-gatherers went from door to door, seeking gossip, family histories, special events to which a family looked forward. Under Turhan's guidance, the staff practiced writing stories in simple language, using basic sentence structure. The only thing holding them back was how to get the first copies printed. They decided if the six of them could copy the letters Turhan wrote for them on a model paper, they could each produce three news-papers a day. In two weeks, that would mean two hundred fifty copies. It would be hard, tedious work, but it could be done.

"How long would it take us to buy a printing press, Turhan Effendim?" one of the men asked as they sat around a table, each writing his own story.

"Let's calculate and see." Turhan started to write numbers on the paper. This was a *concept* the men understood, but it was the first time they'd seen the Arabic numerals. "Suppose we print two hundred fifty copies of our paper, once every month. We sell the paper to the villagers for one *kurush* each. That is two hundred fifty *kurush*, two-and-a-half *lira*. If we sell five printed announcements at ten *kurush* each, that's another half *lira*. We must pay you, our writers, some money, and we'd have to buy paper and pens from Van. That means we could expect to make a profit of one hundred *kurush*, one *lira*, each time the paper comes out. We could probably find a very old, but useable, printing press for one hundred fifty *lira*."

"*Vakh!*" the man remarked in disgust. "It would take twelve years to pay for such a press. We'd be too old to use it when we got it. Even then, what guarantee would we have that such an old press wouldn't break down?"

The group sadly contemplated this cruel fate, when Turhan said, "My friends, are we here to say what *can't* be done, or are we here to make it happen? If *our* work results in an easier life for our sons, isn't it worth doing?" By the hostile glares he received, Turhan concluded it was not the most diplomatic thing he could have said at that moment.

"I've done it! I've done it!" Turhan shouted with glee two weeks later. Early that morning, he'd gone to the home of each of his associates, roused them out of bed, and insisted they go to the village meeting hall immediately. He had unbelievable news for them. An hour later, the men shuffled into the large room.

"Turhan Effendim, you look like a cat that found a mountain of mice," the *muhtar* said. "What's your news?"

"Last week, I went to Van to report back to my superiors. While I was there, I found a fifty-year-old screw-down hand press. The print shop there had just purchased a new electric platen press. The owner was willing to sell his old one for a hundred lira. I bargained him down to sixty."

"So?" the muhtar responded. "It'll still be five years before we can afford it. How is that good news?"

"Ankara directed me to start news-papers. I telegraphed the ministry of information in the capital and told them of our plight. Their response came by wire this morning. I won't read it to you. I want to see who among you can read the best."

A man of twenty-five stepped forward. Turhan handed the tissue-thin paper to him. Pointing to each word, the man read slowly, but clearly, "*Turhan Türkoğlu, stop. Van, stop. The Ministry of Interior is happy to announce that it hereby grants the village of Dorutay fifty lira for a printing press, stop. The government is proud of the people of Dorutay, stop. We are also loaning an additional fifty lira to the village to make sure the news-paper is a success, stop. The village may repay this fifty lira at the rate of five lira each year, stop. May Allah bring your news-paper great success, stop.*"

The man never finished reading the telegram. With a joyous whoop, six men applauded wildly, and ran through the village shouting, "A news-paper, a news-paper! Get ready for a news-paper!"

When the hand press was delivered to Dorutay ten days later, the entire village celebrated the event with an all-night party. Many got drunk on *raki* and nursed severe headaches the following morning. Turhan taught three of the brighter men how to set type. The first proof came off the hand press. Turhan looked at it critically. "Men," he said, "this is a wonderful start. It is almost ready to go. But we must always make sure words are spelled correctly, sentences make sense, and stories are interesting."

They went back to work again. Fatma's baby was almost due. If they waited a few days, they could announce the grand news. Finally, Turhan pronounced the galley proof acceptable. The result was a single page that made history as the first news-paper ever published east of

Van. The lead article was, itself, a masterpiece of direct news reporting and absolute simplicity:

"HAMDI AND FATMA HAVE A BABY GIRL!

There is joy in farmer Hamdi's house. Fatma has a new baby girl. Her name is Nesheli. Mashallah!"

The news-paper even boasted a single advertisement. *"Abdul the tailor sends his greetings. He does good work."*

In all, two hundred fifty copies were printed, one for every man, woman and child in the village, and several more in case anyone in the surrounding areas might want to know what was going on in Dorutay. At that time, Turhan Türkoğlu was already a nationally known journalist and had every reason to expect his success would continue to grow in years to come. Yet, he would never be prouder than the moment he saw his name as first editor on the masthead of a single page newspaper in an insignificant village somewhere near the frontier of Turkey and Iran, "Dorutay Dünya" – the self-proclaimed Dorutay *World*.

4

"Now, *Muhtar* Bey, about the *jirit* lessons you promised?"

"*Jirit* is a winter game. If you want to wait until the new snows fall, we'll gladly teach you. Now that the harvest is in, we play a much more exciting sport, *buz kashı*! In *jirit*, you can be pursued by as many as ten horsemen at any time. In *buz kashı*, it's you against two hundred!"

During the following weeks, Turhan watched practice rounds and learned the rudiments of this mayhem-disguised-as-a-game, brought to Anatolia by Timur Leng's warriors eight centuries before. The game seemed very simple. Two posts were set in the ground, two miles apart. Halfway between them was a marked-off area, ten yards wide by five yards long. The carcass of a dead goat, its head removed, was placed in the "pit," the area in the center. The object of the game was for a rider to come into the "pit," grab the goat carcass, ride to one post, circle it, ride down field to the other post, circle it, and return to the pit, where he then dropped the carcass and scored a point. Two hundred mounted horsemen could be on the field at any given time. Since Dorutay had a population of only two hundred fifty, men from several villages often rode in for a match.

The following Sunday afternoon, Turhan and his news-paper staff, now ten strong, went to the playing field together. They took a lunch of meat, mixed vegetables, bread, and, of course, rakı. Everyone from the village was there. The game could be played in one of two ways, single man or team. In the single man game, whoever had possession of the carcass was the target of every man on the field. In the team contest, two equal teams were chosen. A man would have a hundred allies to assist him in bringing the carcass to the pit.

Buz kashı season lasted from July until the first snows fell. The *muhtar* decreed that the first game of the year would be a team effort. There were two teams of a hundred men to a side, each man riding a small pony. The teams took their places on opposite sides of the field. The *muhtar* placed the goat's carcass in the center of the field, went over to the sidelines and raised a large, old-fashioned muzzle-loading firearm. He pulled the trigger. Two hundred ponies, spurred on by their riders, charged to the center of the field, amidst the spectators' wild cheers. For the first few minutes, there was little more than a blur of action. Horses milled, collided, and separated again. A single horse and rider broke loose from the crowd, making several sharp feints, and headed toward the post a mile to Turhan's left.

The rider was within fifty yards of the post, when a sturdy white horse smashed directly into the right flank of his pony. As the rider steadied himself, a second attacker grabbed the carcass and headed toward the opposite post. The first rider hesitated for an instant, then whirled his steed about and pursued the thief who'd deprived him of the point.

After the first hour, half the players retired from the game. Another hour elapsed. Twenty men and their steeds remained on the field. At sunset, the *muhtar* discharged his firearm a second time, signaling the end of the match. The team on which Turhan had bet a single lira lost five-to-three. By that time he and his friends were so high on *rakı* they didn't care. That evening, the village held a community fête. Most players sported bruises all over their faces and arms. They appeared not to notice their "souvenirs," and spoke of heroics each promised to show in games to come.

The following afternoon, Turhan approached the village headman. Months in the bracing mountain air had hardened his body. He was more eager than ever to learn the game. The *muhtar* called to his son, Ahmet, who was in the next room. When the broad-shouldered young man, ten years Turhan's junior appeared, the muhtar said, proudly, "Ahmet is the best *buz kashı* player in the entire district. I can't think of a better instructor."

"Good afternoon, Effendim," Ahmet said. "I'm pleased you want to learn *buz kashı* and honored my father chose me to help you. First, and most important, we must get you a suitable horse."

One of Ahmet's closest friends maintained four particularly tough ponies, veterans of both *buz kashı* and *jirit* matches. The friend was happy to allow Turhan his choice of the small horses. Turhan picked a small, gray-white stallion, *Savashchı* – Warrior – which looked particularly strong. "A good selection," Ahmet said. "He's the youngest of them all, and will take well to training."

For the next several days, Turhan worked three hours each afternoon with Ahmet and Warrior. Ahmet's instructions were sharp, direct, and constructive. "The horse is a complete extension of you. You must be the master of that single unit. Warrior must anticipate exactly what you want. Don't ever disappoint him. He'll obey you without question, no matter how many horses and riders surround him. He'll charge another horse at full speed. If you don't turn him away at the last moment, he'll ram the other, even if it means his own death. He can reverse direction in two of his own lengths, while he's at full run. He depends entirely on your command."

By the end of the second week, Turhan felt he and Warrior were operating as a team. He asked his trainer whether he was ready. "Not nearly, Effendim. First you must engage in one-on-one practice rounds, then two-on-one, finally ten against you."

"But Ahmet, it'll be *jirit* season before you think I'm ready."

"Perhaps, but *buz kashı* is very dangerous. You have absolutely no protection. You'll be amidst charging horses on every side. The object is not simply to play the game well, but to come out of it alive."

Turhan practiced four hours every day of the week. His body compacted further. He felt as hard as a block of iron. At the beginning of October, the weather turned frosty. This coming Sunday would be the last match of the season. It was tradition in Dorutay that the last game be an "individual" effort.

On Wednesday, the muhtar approached him. "Teacher Effendim, Ahmet says you're ready. On behalf of our village, I invite you to participate in this Sunday's final *buz kashı* match." Turhan could barely conceal his excitement. He was the only *yabanjı*, the only foreigner in recent memory, to be invited to play.

"Remember, no unnecessary chances," Ahmet advised. "You are hero enough, simply for being invited to play the game. If you survive with only a few bruises, you'll be a still greater celebrity. Stay well back in the pack. No matter how capable you think you are, don't try for a goal. Take it easy. Defend. Use this match to learn."

"I will, Ahmet," the journalist said, with every intention of obeying his instructor. He heard a loud outburst, followed by a steady chant, "Turhan! Turhan! Turhan!" He looked over and grinned when he saw his newspaper staff and their families throwing hats in the air, stamping their feet, and eagerly spurring him to action.

The *muhtar* fired his gun. The match began. Turhan kept Warrior well back of the center group. During the first thirty minutes, his mount did little more than gallop up and down the field, trailing all but a few of the other riders. He felt more at ease as the tourney progressed. Several horses and players dropped out. Warrior was not even breathing heavily. Thus far, the *buz kashı* game had been nothing more than a brisk ride in the country. Ahmet was the only man on the field who'd scored a goal. An angry blue welt over his right eye showed that nothing was gained in this contest without sacrifice.

Turhan loped along toward the rear of the pack. Suddenly, from out of nowhere, the carcass was hurtled in his direction and struck him in the right shoulder. He reached out involuntarily to stop its fall, and brought it close to his saddle. There was an explosive roar from the crowd, cries of "Turhan! Turhan! Turhan!" The nearest post was less than forty yards away. He couldn't let this opportunity pass him by. He'd practiced the twists and turns Ahmet had taught him. Now, he and Warrior used them. Miraculously, the distance widened between himself and the riders nearest him. Warrior felt the electric excitement and pounded toward the first stake, moving without the need of command. Turhan no longer heard the cheers. Everything seemed to move in slow motion. He circled the stake. Warrior, sensing the open field ahead, broke into a full run. The second post was half a mile away, a quarter mile away. Pandemonium erupted on both sides of the field. He and Warrior were a hundred yards from the goalpost, fifty, twenty-five. For just an instant, he had the sensation of being hit by an express train. That was his last conscious thought.

5

"Perhaps they could have saved time and simply agreed at the beginning of the game to sever your head and use it as the *buz kashı* carcass." The voice came from deep down a well.

"Nadji?"

"None other, my friend. Several years ago, you and Halide arranged for my transportation to a hospital. I've just returned the favor."

"Where am I?"

"Third District Military Hospital. Diyarbakır."

Turhan struggled to full consciousness. His left arm was in a cast. "What happened?"

"What did your friend Ahmet tell you? Don't try to make a goal in your first game? Make sure you leave the field in one piece?"

"I remember now," Turhan replied. "The carcass was there. I couldn't help myself. By the way, did I ever make it to the goal?"

"No. The carcass spun out just before you were clobbered from both sides."

"Allah! What about Warrior?"

141

"He fell on top of you. Broke both your legs, but fortunately not his. The *muhtar* arranged for a relay team of horses to go to the frontier guard post at Saray, where they had access to the telegraph. The army took care of getting you to Van, where the provincial hospital determined you had a severe concussion, a broken arm and two broken legs. I was in Mardin at the time, and asked that the military fly you here so I could see if you really were as indestructible as they said."

Shortly afterward, Halide strode determinedly into Turhan's room, accompanied by a young woman in her mid-twenties with a pleasant, open face, brown eyes, and mid-length dark hair. "What's this all about?" Halide berated him. "Are we wagering among ourselves who'll be the first to depart this Earth? Who do you think you are, Ghengiz Khan?"

Turhan grinned sheepishly and nodded in the direction of Halide's companion. "Forgive me, Turhan," Halide continued without pause, as though she'd not even noticed his look. "As I grow older, I forget my once fine, French manners. May I introduce you to Sezer, my second-in-command. Like you, she's a villager who came to the city to make something of her life."

"I'm pleased to meet you, Sezer Hanım. I'd reach over and shake your hand, but I'm indisposed." What an attractive young woman, he thought. Could this be one of those thousands of Turkish village women emerging into the Twentieth Century that Jalal had talked about?

During the next week, Halide, Nadji, and Sezer returned daily to visit Turhan. On Friday, his two friends told him they were convinced he'd survive and they intended to go about their business elsewhere. Sezer would be staying in Diyarbakır, preparing for the next influx of teacher candidates. The following day she returned to the hospital alone, and brought flowers to cheer up Turhan's room.

"Do you need anything from the outside world?" she asked.

"I wonder if you could find a copy of the new novel by the American author Ernest Hemingway?"

"*The Sun Also Rises*?" she replied. "I'll certainly try."

"You've read the book?" he asked, pleasantly surprised at her astuteness.

"No." She looked at the floor, then said, "I teach at a basic level. I'm still very much a student. I'm learning more each day. Would it be too much if I asked you to read it aloud to me?"

"Only if you hold the book for me."

When Turhan left the hospital, he continued to help Sezer with her lessons. Within a month, she could read most of the currently available books by herself. When their afternoons together abated, he found to his surprise that he missed her.

One day, she arrived with a package wrapped in red and white paper. "I bought this for you with my own money," she said, proudly. "It's not a novel, but a new play, from America. I thought you'd like it."

He unwrapped the gift. His eyes widened with pleasure as he read the title, "The Front Page," by Ben Hecht and Charles MacArthur.

"Halide told me you're a newspaper-man. I thought you'd like to read about newspaper-men in other countries."

"Thank you, Sezer Hanım," he said, deeply touched. "You seem to know my tastes better than anyone. Yet, I know nothing about you."

"There's not much to tell. I never knew my parents. As long as I can remember, I washed clothes, threshed wheat, and swept out huts, in order to eat. I learned to exist on rice and vegetables, sometimes overripe, nearly rotting fruit. If you cut around the bad parts, it tastes as sweet as the best quality. When Halide came to our village, I saw a chance to escape. I had no dowry. No man was willing to claim me as his wife. Some boys wanted to fool around with me behind the village hill. When they found out I wasn't that kind, no one really cared whether I lived or died.

"I don't earn a great deal working for Halide – five lira a month – but it's so much more than I've ever earned in my life it's a fortune to me. I don't need much. Food is cheap in Diyarbakır if you're willing to wait 'til the end of the day to buy. I pay so little for my room I'm able to save one lira a month. Eventually, I'll have enough for my own dowry. If I'm too old to marry by then, I'll always be able to support myself and not burden any man."

Turhan looked at the book she'd purchased for him. The price was two lira – two months toward her dowry gone.

The next day, they walked around the city together. He talked about his own background. Sezer was interested in everything he had to say. "I've had such a wonderful day," she said to him. "I wish it would never end." She smiled at him. He realized, not for the first time, how attractive she was. "Listen," she said. "Would you like to come to dinner tonight? It'll be a very simple meal. The room where I'm staying is not much to look at, but you're certainly welcome."

The invitation caused Turhan to realize how lonely for a woman's companionship – indeed for anyone's evening company – he'd been these last few weeks. While he enjoyed reading and sometimes prowled the city's streets, it had become boring. He looked eagerly forward to the time when the doctors would pronounce him fit to travel again.

"I'd be delighted to come," he replied, "but only if you allow me to bring some kebabs."

She blushed. "Is something the matter?" he asked.

"I've not had any meat since I've been in Diyarbakır. I'd never presume to ask such a thing of you."

"Don't presume, my lady. Tonight you shall dine on the best lamb you've ever eaten!"

During dinner, they were unusually polite, more subdued than they'd been with one another in the past. They were also beginning to appreciate things about the other they'd not observed before. Turhan took his leave much later than his normal bedtime, walking home slowly, thoughtfully.

After he left, Sezer retired to her small bed chamber. She took out a rarely used mirror. She'd never been a vain girl. Now, peering into its depths, she saw that her face had high color. Was this pretty young woman really Sezer, the orphan from Suvarli? She undressed slowly, taking careful stock of herself. She had fine, firm, upstanding breasts. Given the opportunity, they would feed many sons someday, *Inshallah*. Unconsciously, her hands wandered over her smooth body. As she lay back in her bed, her thoughts went directly to Turhan. Repeating his name over and over, she soon fell into a deep, blissful sleep.

During the following week, they saw each other every day. Dinners became a habit, sometimes at his apartment or a restaurant, most often in her small room. They spoke of everything except what each was beginning to feel inside. When Turhan told Sezer he'd be traveling on government business for the next month, she said she understood perfectly. She herself needed to meet Halide in Urfa to discuss recruitment strategies for the coming year.

Turhan ran across Halide three weeks later, when their paths crossed at Sivrek. "I've spent the last two weeks with Sezer," she said.

"I know," Turhan replied. She told me she was going to meet with you."

"She's in love with you, you know."

"She's *what?*"

"You heard me."

Turhan was taken aback by Halide's directness. "We're quite friendly and all, but..."

"Listen, Turhan. You're thirty-two, same as me. You're not getting any younger. A girl like Sezer doesn't come along every day. It's time for you to marry, my friend."

"Marry? Did I hear you say marry?"

"That's exactly the word I used. Do you think you'll do any better than Sezer? A girl who'll be the best helpmate you could ever hope to have? I've worked with her day and night for a year-and-a-half. I know."

"But...?"

"Do what you want, my friend. If you have a shred of intelligence in that thick head of yours, I'll soon be attending a wedding. If not, that's your problem."

There was only one person in whom he could confide. As he and Jalal walked along the banks of the Tigris, outside Diyarbakır, he thought back to a time so many years ago when his mentor had patiently listened, then given sound advice. In the gathering autumn, the river was little more than a sluggish stream. From here, Diyarbakır looked no different than it had the first time he'd seen it. The timeless basalt walls, surrounded by scrub steppe, hid the modern city inside. The old man was still able to outpace Turhan during the first fifteen minutes of the walk. Turhan broke the silence more quickly than during their first foray. "I give up, Jalal effendi. If you keep going, you'll have solved my problem readily. I'll simply fall over and die from exhaustion."

"A good, spirited walk clears the cobwebs from the mind, boy. Gives you a chance to organize your thoughts. Besides, the old tea house is still where it's been when last we walked this path." Half an hour later, each nursed a glass of tea while looking out over the dry plain. "All right, Turhan. Who's the young lady? And you don't have to look down at the ground. That was fine when you were thirteen."

"Your gentle, understanding ways are overwhelming."

"That's never been our relationship, and you know it."

"Her name is Sezer. She's Halide's assistant, a girl from Suvarli village. She's quite a bit younger than me. Halide says she's in love with me."

"How do you feel toward her?"

"Compassion. She's an orphan and was an outcast in her village."

"Aha! The Turhan of Suvarli, in shawl and shalvar." The old man chuckled.

"It's not funny, Jalal Effendim."

"I'm not laughing at you, Turhan. It's the situation."

"What do you mean?"

"Tell me a little more about this girl."

"She never really had a chance in her village. Scullery maid, field laborer. She's known nothing but work all her life. The boys thought she was good for only one thing, but she tells me she refused all their advances. Her life would have been nothing, the smallest mote on the meanest, least consequential dot of earth ever created by Allah. One day, Halide came to her village and she started to learn. She never compromised her morals to enable her to get ahead."

"Are you in love with her?"

"What does it mean to love?"

"Are you serious?"

"Never more so in my life."

"Very well. Let's take a look at your experiences with women. Take Gönül, for one. Don't look embarrassed, you asked me what love is. I'm trying to help you find the answer you seek. When you met Gönül, she was older and married. You enjoyed the sexual connection, but you obviously knew she was using you as much as you were using her. She dazzled you by her wealth and her apparent experience. Have you been with other women since?"

"Nothing I'd call significant, Effendim."

"What does Halide think about this?"

"She wants me to marry to Sezer tomorrow."

Jalal rose, paid the tea house bill, and beckoned Turhan follow him. They forded the stream and sat in the shade of a sparse growth of trees on the other side. "It's nearly impossible to explain love," Jalal continued, "You can't talk about it with the same detachment you'd reserve for cutting a lamb carcass into component parts, Turhan. You want me to answer a question that has baffled men and women since the world began. I will make some observations. Don't interrupt me until I'm finished, all right."

"As you say, Effendim."

"I believe you're attracted to Sezer, else why would you even have asked my advice. Sezer apparently had a background remarkably similar to that of your mother. However, instead of walking the street of shame, she's taken a noble path. She's suffered much the same as you when you were young, and she's risen above her humble beginnings, just like you. Sezer offers you respectability in your own eyes. Unquestionably 'society' would like to see you marred. It's time you were fathering sons. It's clear you admire the girl. Do you need respectability because you associated in the past with those you thought may have been less than respectable?"

Turhan glanced sharply at the old man. Jalal continued, as if the look had been nothing more than a fly buzzing about his head. "I'm seventy-two years old, Turhan. I've been married twice, had several casual liaisons in between, and, more important, I do not consider myself naïve. Ibrahim smuggled drugs and weapons, just as did the Agha Khorusun and the Agha Nikrat. You are not tainted by your association with them, even though you might believe otherwise." Turhan thought back to that desperately unhappy time when Nadji had brought up the specter of his past. "It's clear that all your previous experiences with women have not prepared you for love, else you would never have needed my counsel. The only positive relationships you've had with women are those where it was not necessary to give of yourself emotionally.

"So now you're faced with something new, something different, and you don't know quite how to deal with it. Sezer, I take it, is physically attractive to you?"

"Yes."

"She comes from the same humble beginnings as you. She is 'safe' in that she'll never compete with you intellectually. She inhabits your world but won't inhibit you. And Halide, whose approval you seek more than any other person, is urging you to marry her."

"Yes. You've told me all the positive reasons to marry Sezer."

"But that may not be enough."

"What do you mean, Effendim?"

"Most human beings never stop to analyze love. That's why, for centuries, parents have arranged marriages for their children. Love is an imponderable, probably the worst reason in the world to marry, although it's worked pretty well for me. You don't have parents to arrange a marriage for you. Neither does Sezer, so the two of you are left to your own devices. Still, whether you admit it or not, you want the approval of those closest to you.

"Maybe you're the kind who needs to marry for that very reason. But you'd better realize some of the dangers when someone of your character embarks on such a journey. You are an intensely ambitious man, Turhan. You've shown that by the successes you've achieved in such a limited time. You don't really care about worldly honors or wealth, although they seem to have come to you early. Rather, you need to affect the world you live in.

"Several months ago, you told me Halide might as well be married to Turkey. You're really no different. As long as I've known you, you've been bound to the never-ending search for truth, the all-abiding desire to see that the little man achieves justice. That's admirable, Turhan. But I question whether you will ever allow yourself fully to give your heart to another human being."

Turhan stared straight at his earliest mentor.

"On the surface, everything about marriage to Sezer is objectively 'correct.' You are more than old enough to marry. You're intelligent enough to realize that Sezer can help you achieve greater maturity than you could ever attain without her. She's a 'good' girl and a 'safe' one, perhaps the first for whom you've ever sensed an attraction. On that level, Turhan, you may well be 'in love' with this girl. But before you commit yourself one way or the other, look inside yourself. Are being fair to her? If not, you'll be undermining the very essence of your being."

That night, and for many thereafter, Turhan thought about the old man's words. Love? How could he explain the concept? Yet he'd seen how intensely Halide had loved Metin. Nadji was married to a stunningly beautiful woman. Who wouldn't be in love with Aysheh? They were the perfect match for one another. Both had the good looks, breeding, background, class, and flawless ease which assured success in everything they undertook, and they obviously adored one another.

Sezer was a pretty woman. She possessed everything he'd ever really wanted in a mate. Sensibility and sensitivity. Thoughtfulness and goodness. Courage and a safe harbor for his emotions. Jalal was both right and wrong. He was right in causing Turhan to think more deeply about the concept of love. But, Turhan convinced himself, Jalal was wrong when he said Turhan could not give love to another human being.

Several nights later, Turhan invited Sezer to an extravagant meal he'd prepared himself. Afterward, they gazed with frank longing at one another. Neither knew who ventured the first gentle kiss. Shortly afterward, their kisses turned more passionate. Turhan turned off the lights. They continued kissing. Then, their explorations became more direct. That night, Sezer did not sleep in her room on Kurtalan Street.

Sezer had had no previous experience in lovemaking, but she was strong, healthy, eager to give pleasure and take it. Before long, she was as adept at this wonderful new game as any who'd ever played it. When, at dawn, their bodies were sated with one another, they collapsed into happily exhausted slumber. They did not awake until late in the afternoon. It was time to make love again.

Halide had predicted that they'd marry by late spring, but they wed earlier. In February, 1930, Turhan and Sezer were united in a civil ceremony conducted by the mayor of Diyarbakır. The announcement of their marriage was duly reported in two newspapers. Turhan kept both of them. The first, of course, was *Isharet*. The second didn't reach him until many months later. But the story was given much more prominence in the second paper. In fact, it was the lead article on the front – and only – page of the Dorutay *World*.

During the first six months of their marriage, Sezer and Turhan worked successfully together in a number of villages. Their achievements propelled them to greater heights. They had little opportunity for undisturbed time with one another, for by day's end they were exhausted and each tomorrow presented a new challenge. Sezer was proud of her man's accomplishments and never tired of telling him so. Her greatest strength lay in her simple country background. Sezer was a hungry, demanding lover, but all too soon Turhan's ardor seemed to cool. In the past, he'd always been excited by the forbidden aspects of sex, the ability to conquer the unattainable. Now, he was involved in a committed relationship with a woman who was not only readily available, but who viewed lovemaking as only one part of their life. As eager to satisfy as she was, Sezer was not the stuff of which fantasies were made.

Sezer sensed that Turhan was distancing himself from the very intimacy she hungered for most. At first, she simply accepted Turhan's behavior as typical of a man. She respected Turhan too much to voice her anger. With the exception of Halide, she'd known rejection all of her life. It was the way of the world that people never really got what they wanted.

A little more than a year after they'd been married, Turhan realized that Jalal had spoken the truth when he'd said it might well be impossible for him fully to love another human being. He felt guilty, for he knew Sezer was giving him much more love than he deserved. But it was not within him to reach out, to say the accepting word, to touch her with the magic combination of gentleness and desire. Their marriage settled into a life of two compatible friends occupying the same bed but different worlds. While they provided periodic sexual satisfaction to one another, it was dutiful, a pleasurable if somewhat mechanical act. They determined this would not be the right time for children. Each had so much to accomplish. Turhan extended his trips in the east. Sezer found herself working more and more with Halide.

Turhan and Sezer frequently invited Halide to dine with them. Neither Turhan nor Sezer ever mentioned dissatisfaction with the marriage to Halide. They never spoke with one another about it. Each simply assumed, silently, that this was the way marriage was supposed to be. When it was time for Turhan to return to Ankara, Turhan and Sezer had settled down to what they'd accepted as reasonable contentment with their lot.

6

"So you're leaving Diyarbakır, too?" Turhan asked Nadji. They'd met in a tea house the afternoon before the journalist and his wife were to leave for Ankara."

"I am. I thought I'd finished my obligation to the Gazi, but I guess not. He's sending me out to Doğubayezit to bring more young boys into today's world. If it's anything like the past year, it'll be enlightening. I swear, the way these young soldiers drive trucks you'd think they were *almost* ready for the wheel. They're doing a little better when I insist they eat with forks and knives." Nadji chuckled.

"So you're going to be the next Noah?" Turhan chided.

"Not quite. Doğubayezit army base is a good hundred and fifty kilometers from the base of *Ağrı Dağ*, Mount Ararat. They say the wind never stops blowing off the mountain."

"What does Aysheh say about all this?"

"'No, thank you.' She's not happy that I'll be gone, but it's only a three month assignment, and then we've been promised Izmir. I suggested she might use the time I'm gone to visit her sister in Istanbul, and she thought that was a good idea."

154

"What about her parents?"

"They're still in Washington. They've extended his tour of duty as the ambassador. He wrote us that he doesn't think Mr. Hoover will run for another term as President and there's a lot of talk about a fellow named Franklin Roosevelt. The name means nothing to me."

They finished their tea and Turhan ordered two more glasses. "How's the general?" They both knew he was talking about Nadji's father, not the Gazi.

"He retired two months ago, three years after he got his second star."

"So he really did become a pasha," Turhan mused.

"I haven't heard that honorific title since the collapse of the Ottoman Empire eight years ago. Mama was so proud of him, but now that he's sixty-one she complains he's underfoot all the time."

"They could travel the world."

"Yes, but they did a lot of that during his thirty years in the Army."

"So what does he do with his spare time, now that there's lots of it?"

"He probably spends half his time polishing that big old Mercedes. Would you believe the Gazi was at his retirement and actually gave him his choice of the Mercedes or a gold watch?"

"They couldn't have thought of a better gift," Turhan said. "I imagine his pension keeps him in petrol." Turhan paid the tab, and the two men walked into Diyarbakır's main square. "What'll you be doing in Izmir, Nadji?"

"They're assigning me to the Army's diplomatic school, after which time I pin on the silver leaves of a *yarbay* – a lieutenant colonel – and they'll dispatch me to duty as a military attaché at one of our embassies."

"Quite an early promotion, my friend. With Aysheh being a diplomat's daughter as well as being beautiful and socially adept, it looks like you've got the perfect future ahead."

"Inshallah. What about you, Turhan? Back to *Isharet*'s Ankara bureau?"

"Probably. But whatever happens, I look forward to big city life again. Have you heard anything about our Halide? Her two years of service are coming to an end, too."

"As a matter of fact, I have. She's made not-so-subtle suggestions to our glorious leader that he could carry his ambitious programs much farther, much faster, if there were a Turkish college to train teachers. She's spoken with the administrators of Robert College, the American institution in Istanbul, and they've got some excess land they'd sell her at a very good price. My guess is that the Gazi will find a way to fund the teachers' college. It seems he's been particularly generous to those who took him up on his challenge to bring Turkey into the twentieth century. Which is why I asked what you think is in store for you.

When Turhan returned to the capital, he was amazed at the changes he saw. His two years in the southeast had hardly prepared him for the sight of a large number of unveiled young women, wearing clothing of the type he saw in the European magazines now openly displayed on newsstands. Women strolled leisurely on the wide sidewalks of Ankara's main thoroughfare, often unaccompanied by men.

When he overheard casual conversations in several cafes dotting Yenishehir, Ankara's "new city," he learned just how profound Kemal's revolution had been. When he'd left the capital in 1928, Mustafa Kemal had instituted the previously unheard-of concept of competing political parties. Now, it seemed, the *Gazi* had concluded Turkey was not ready for responsible opposition, and had ordered the Free Republican Party to disband. If Kemal was not yet a god, he was certainly a monument.

But the leader's consolidation of power did not stifle angry voices of dissent. While the entrenched clergy dared not appear in the Allah-damned nationalist capital, its reactionary voice was reflected in furtive glances, whispers, and embarrassed silences of those recently arrived from the villages, who brought their traditions on their backs. Those men made certain *their* women wore shawls and shalvar. They continued to carry small prayer rugs with them and made obeisance by bowing toward Mecca five times each day, despite snickers and derisive comments made by "sophisticates."

Early in 1931, Mustafa Kemal summoned Turhan to the presidential office for a private talk. "Turhan, the government recently erected a radio broadcasting unit in Ankara. We're having difficulties getting started. We've no way of knowing what the people in the towns and villages want to hear. You've spent the last two years traveling all over the eastern part of the country. Could you put together a series of programs that might appeal to the Turkish people?"

"Another 'assignment', Excellency?"

"Consider it more of an opportunity, my friend. Of course, if you're not interested, I could ask Refik, *Milliyet's* popular columnist."

"As usual, Gazi, you make a compelling argument."

"*Akshamlarınız hayırlı olsun*! Good evening, my friends! This is Turhan Türkoğlu calling on *Radio Ankara*, the Voice of Turkey. I hope you have had a wonderful day. May Allah bless your rest. It's time for the news! Turhan's gruff, instantly recognizable voice, appealed to Turks in every walk of life.

Within a month, his evening program of current events, candid observations, music, and advice, which ran from six to ten each night, was Turkey's most popular radio show. By the end of 1932, two years after his return to the capital, he was one of Turkey's best known personalities. Some of this was due to *Isharet's* growth, but his greatest popularity came because more people listened to Turhan than listened to Kemal himself.

The president stopped in at least once a week, and usually stayed late. One night, at the beginning of 1933, the Gazi was in a mellow mood when he entered the studio, having already quaffed half a bottle of Chivas Regal scotch. "Turhan," he said. "Your influence in Turkey is almost as great as mine. I feel fortunate indeed that you've spoken favorably of my plans on your evening programs."

"Gazi, no one respects you more than I. But you know I'll always speak my mind, no matter the consequence. If I don't agree with your ideas, I'll say so."

"What if I don't approve of your views?"

"You have three choices. You order me to resign, you fire me, or you choke on what I say and listen respectfully."

"Bravo, Turhan! You're one of the few who's ever disagreed with me and still kept your job."

"Not to mention my head, Gazi!"

The two men laughed. Kemal poured Turhan a drink from the open bottle. The evening broadcast had concluded half an hour before. Kemal felt like playing poker. Turhan roused three press colleagues, one English, one American, one German, from the nearby Ankara

Palas Hotel. As the night wore on, drinks flowed and tongues loosened considerably. It was tacitly agreed that what they said that night would not go outside the studio.

"Grundig, what in holy Hell is going to happen to Europe, now that you've put that postcard painter in office?"

"God only knows, Mister President," the German responded affably. "Hitler *did* get elected by popular democratic vote."

"Don't give me that crap, Otto!" the American interrupted him with a loud belch. "That Nazi's got some strange ideas. Have you read *Mein Kampf?*"

"Natürlich, Mike, that's required reading now."

"Do you buy into those ideas?"

"Politicians spout whatever they think will get them elected. No offense, Mr. President."

"None taken, Otto. Your Führer wants me to accredit a reporter from *Völkischer Beobachter* to Ankara."

"I say, Kemal, surely you wouldn't allow that rag here?"

"No, Percy, you don't have to worry about that, but I'm afraid you'll soon have a lot to worry about up in your part of the continent."

"We've got treaties with the buggers," the Englishman replied. "That's one thing the Jerries understand."

"You think so?" the President asked. "After the Great War ended, the Allies tried to impose their will on Turkey. Turhan and I were in Istanbul at the time. It was a pretty grim place. I remember saying, back in 1919, that if Turkey were pushed to the wall, we'd throw all foreigners out. That's exactly what happened. You Allies forced a pretty harsh peace on Germany. The economic depression hasn't made anyone particularly friendly toward one another. They say that until recently inflation was so rampant in Germany you brought a wheelbarrow full of money into a bakery to buy a loaf of bread."

"I remember those days," the German replied. "At one time, the *mark* was two *trillion* to the dollar. You did better to wipe your arse with banknotes than use them for anything else."

"I'd watch Germany very closely were I in your shoes," Kemal said. "That crazy man who's come to power may well pull the trigger that blows the head off Europe."

"Easy, fellows," the American rejoined. "Here we are, watching our friend Kemal drag a country from the Middle Ages to the twentieth century in the span of ten years. I propose a toast! *Sherefinize*! Good health and long life to you, Mr. President!"

"Hear, hear!" the four comrades agreed.

As dawn broke over the capital, the foreigners left the studio. Kemal and Turhan stayed on, talking quietly in a small, private office. "You've been married how long, Turhan, three years next month, I believe?" Although the president had consumed copious quantities of Scotch whisky during the night, and had undoubtedly been awake nearly twenty-four hours, Turhan was amazed at Kemal's recall of the slightest details.

"Precisely, Gazi. Why do you ask?"

"One would have thought you'd have had two sons by now." He chuckled gently as he saw Turhan's discomfort. "Never mind, my friend. I know how it is. Since Halide started Yujel Orhan Teacher's College last year, Sezer's probably been in Istanbul more than she's been home. The Germans used to have a saying with regard to their women, '*kirche, küche, kinder*' – church, kitchen and children.' Maybe I've gone too far with this women's rights thing?"

"Whether you have or haven't is not for me to judge. The clock's moved forward."

"Indeed. How are things between you and Sezer, by the way?"

"Fine. Why shouldn't they be? Her work's as important as mine. We're both fulfilled..."

"And children?" the president asked again.

"When the time's right, there'll be sons, Gazi. We both knew there'd be work to do first."

"And you're obviously enjoying yours?"

"You'd know I was lying if I said I didn't. Who'd have thought a thirty-six-year-old bumpkin from a little village in southeastern Turkey would be rubbing elbows with the president of his country, poking fun at international politicians, and getting paid well for it?"

"Who, indeed? Turhan, how would you like an opportunity to do even more than that?"

"What do you mean, Gazi?"

As the president unfolded his plan to Turhan, the reporter's eyes widened. What Kemal proposed would change his life. But the situation was fraught with danger. Further, it meant putting his career ahead of his wife's, and he wondered how they'd both be able to deal with that. Sezer was an intelligent woman, with a basic education in language skills. At heart, she was still a simple country girl from Suvarli, whose life work was to bring elementary skills to villagers. Had Turhan himself ever shaken the image of his humble beginnings?

"A year, Turhan, that's all I'm asking of you."

"I'd have to ask Sezer. Why me? To use your own phrase, 'Of course you could ask Refik at *Milliyet*.'"

"I'm serious, Turhan. There's talk I've thrown all my old friends out of Turkey and turned into a crusty dictator just like the rest. I'm not banishing you, *arkadash*. You're one of the few truthful observers I've got left on my side."

"But just last evening you said..."

"That Hitler may start a war if the western powers and the Russians don't stop them. Turhan, they say Berlin is one of the most beautiful and cosmopolitan cities in the world. Before the last war, it was the capital of European culture. I think you'll find it a unique experience."

"And Sezer?"

"She must go with you, of course. It always looks more respectable. That will stop them from thinking there's a 'terrible Turk' coming to kidnap one of their Aryan fräuleins."

"I'd need time to convince her, Gazi. I doubt if she'll be pleased."

"Turhan, remember, you're the man in the relationship. The one in charge."

Now it was Turhan's turn to laugh. "Am I hearing what I think I'm hearing from the champion of rights for all Turks? The man who publicly said, 'Progress is impossible when half our nation stays chained to the kitchen, the veil, the home, while the other half reaches for the skies?'"

"Yes, ahem, well, what we say publicly is one thing..."

"Easy for you to say, Gazi. You're not married. The whole nation is your bride."

"As it is yours, Turhan, whether you know it or not. And I'm asking you to love that bride as much as you love your own."

"How fast could you get me out of Berlin if there were trouble?"

"What makes you think there'll be trouble?"

"Call it 'newsman's intuition.' From what I've heard, I don't think anyone will be able to give an honest opinion of anything in Germany and get away with it."

7

Although Ankara had grown by leaps and bounds, Istanbul, the decaying Ottoman capital, was still "the City," and would always be. At Kemal's insistence, Turhan and Sezer were ensconced, at government expense, in a suite on the fifth floor of the Pera Palas hotel, in the heart of the European district. Turhan had visited the Pera's elegant oak-and-gilt public rooms before, but he'd never actually stayed there. The opulence, so foreign to anything Sezer had ever known, overwhelmed her. "We can't possibly stay in such a place when Turkish villagers are starving. Why can't we simply take lodging in one of the dormitories at the college and tell Mustafa Kemal to use the money for better purpose?"

"And insult the president? Don't worry, darling, the Gazi knows what he's doing. I'm certain the hotel management is contributing most of what it would ordinarily charge, for the good of the nation."

"Actually, I'm proud our country can produce something as elegant as this."

"That's not entirely true."

163

"What do you mean?"

"The founder of Wagons-Lits, George Nagelmackers, built it because fifty years ago he didn't think there was a place luxurious enough for his Grand European Express. It's housed kings and prime ministers, actors and even whores since that time," Turhan laughed.

"Turhan!" Sezer said in mock indignation. She relented, then expressed surprise as she saw her husband pour two flutes of champagne, which had been provided compliments of the management. She felt a warm glow. Perhaps there was still life in the marriage after all.

"To us!" he toasted.

"To us!" she repeated. After she'd taken two small sips, she said, "All right, husband. What's this all about? The president wouldn't have sent you here just for being his star broadcast personality. Kemal wants something."

"You're right, Sezer." He looked at his wife, trying to picture in his mind how she'd appear to the Aryans in Berlin. A pretty country woman. Certainly not their idea of Germanic perfection. Sezer was almost as tall as Turhan, with tawny skin, gentle, alert brown-black eyes, and dark hair knotted in back. Her figure was becoming matronly although she did her best to conceal it. *Kirche, küche, kinder.* "Kemal wants us to go to Berlin for a year."

"Berlin, Germany?"

"Yes."

Sezer said nothing for several moments. She bit down hard on her thumb. Finally, she asked, "Must you go?"

"Weren't you listening, Sezer? Kemal wants *us* to go."

"I heard you, husband," she said, quietly. "Do we have a choice?"

"What do you mean, 'choice'?" he said, raising his voice slightly. "This is the opportunity of a lifetime. We've never been out of Turkey.

This is our chance to see something more than a poor, struggling country. Berlin's the cultural center of the world."

"Turkey's a world of its own," she rejoined with equal fervor. "We are building something here, not tearing things down like Hitler wants to do. There's a place for everyone. We need every man and woman to make it happen. Why do we need to go to a place like that?"

"Because the Gazi demands it."

"I'm your wife, Turhan. I'm entitled to demands of my own. Like a secure, comfortable life right here at home."

Although he spoke quietly, Turhan spoke with a barely concealed threat he'd never dared voice in the past. "Sezer, I would like to have a secure, comfortable life for us right here in Turkey. I would like to have a wife waiting for me each night when I come home. I would like to have sons, although we promised each other it would be a while. But that isn't the life we lead. You're away more than you're in Ankara. When you're not in some dormitory in Istanbul, the whole country is your home. When I'm not writing for *Isharet*, I'm on the air. For better or worse, that's the way our life is at the moment. The Gazi has virtually ordered me to go to Berlin as his private emissary. He didn't give me any choice in the matter. Nor can I give you one."

"And if I choose not to go?"

Silence hung between them like a thick, black cloud. The mood of gaiety had been shattered. Finally, Turhan broke the tense silence. "Let's go have dinner, shall we? Istiklal Caddesi's not far from here."

She nodded, but said nothing.

Istiklal Caddesi was European Istanbul's main artery. Although Turhan's friends from the international press had told him it could never hope to compete with *Unter den Linden*, the *Champs Elysee*, or Piccadilly Circus, Turhan had no basis for comparison. High-fashion

European shops sat cheek-by-jowl with pushcart peddlers who sold barbecued lamb's intestines, pistachio nuts, shish kebabs and fried fish. Within a three block stroll, one could find an Armenian church, an Italian basilica, a Spanish chapel, the Palace of France, and a Chinese restaurant. When Turhan had been a bachelor, he'd loved the rowdy nightclubs and restaurants near *Cicek Passaj* – the Flower Passage – where, for a very few lira, he could sample *mezerler* – Turkish hors d'oeuvres – guzzle beer, enjoy an evening of fellowship with the international press corps, and, should one be so inclined, sample other, more exotic entertainments.

Tonight his mood was somber. He chose the *Yeni Rejans*, a Russian restaurant at the end of a dark, dingy passageway off Lower Istiklal. He'd been there several times before. After the Russian revolution, several ladies, one who'd been a ballerina in Kiev, pooled what little funds they'd had and started the restaurant. Displaced Russian nobles had made it a popular place for Europeans, but the prices were steep for most Istanbulus. Over borscht and breaded veal cutlets, Turhan changed his tone. "I'm sorry I raised my voice earlier, darling," he began. "The Gazi says this is critically important to Turkey. And he promises it's only for a year."

"Then why couldn't you go alone? We've been separated for weeks at a time already. I'm sure he'd let you come back to Istanbul any time you wanted. *Deutsche Lufthansa's* had air service between Berlin and Istanbul since last year. It would take you no time at all to travel between cities."

"Kemal wants us to go as a couple. He says the Germans are very rigid when it comes to propriety. They believe a man should have a wife, and that married couples should function as a unit."

"You mean they don't want a Turk touching their precious Aryan women? Don't look so shocked, I'm just teasing you."

"It's not a joke, Sezer. Kemal said much the same thing to me."

"And for this, you ask me to turn my life upside down with no warning and you expect me to follow you happily to a strange country. I'm not as sophisticated as you. I never will be. But I have learned to read newspapers. I even listen to 'The Voice of Turkey' every night. Somehow I don't believe Berlin is paradise on earth for any but blond-haired Germans."

Turhan's patina of civility was rapidly dissolving. When he spoke, it was in measured tones. "Perhaps you've been listening too much to the modern ideas everyone seems to be spouting. You are my wife, Sezer. Do you forget where you'd have been without me?"

"Without you?" She glared at him. "Without you?" she repeated. "I'd be exactly where I am now, doing exactly what I'm doing today. Building Turkey. Helping the best friend you've ever had. The best friend our nation's ever had, and I include your Gazi when I say that. "Halide Orhan doesn't go around making fancy speeches. She doesn't rub elbows with kings, ministers and presidents, or actors or whores for that matter. Was it *you* who plucked me from the village, Turhan? Or was it Halide who gave me a life beyond the starvation and misery of Suvarli? You are my husband, my man, and I owe you a wifely duty because of it. But don't talk to me about debt. I owe Halide no lesser loyalty than I owe you. The Ankara Radio may be your sacred trust, your first child. Yujel Orhan Teacher's College is mine. Am I any less than you because I'm a mere woman? Well? *Am I?*" She closed her eyes. When she opened them, they were bright with unshed tears, but they were tears of defiance, not tenderness.

Turhan quickly paid the tab. They said nothing to one another on the walk home. Despite their plush accommodations and the deliberately cultured romantic atmosphere of the Pera Palas, they slept in separate beds that night, their feelings as flat as the champagne they'd never bothered to drink.

When he awoke next morning, Sezer was gone. She'd left a brief note. "I'm going to the school. I need to talk to Halide."

Turhan looked out the window. It was gray and sleety. A light patina of slushy snow covered Istanbul's hills. Normally, Turhan would have ridden the Tünel, Istanbul's ancient, one-stop subway, down the hill from the Pera Palas to the Galata Bridge, walked across the dual level span to Eminönü landing, and taken the ferry up the Bosphorous. Today, reacting from anger and injured pride, he hired a taxicab to take him up the narrow Bosphorous coast road. It took two hours for the cab to reach Ortaköy, ten miles north of the city.

The village was situated in a wooded area that hid both the noise and the bustle of Istanbul. The cab dropped him at the foot of a muddy path just beyond the village center. He trudged half a mile up the trail through scrub forest until he came to an opening a few hundred feet above Ortaköy, where the school was located.

Yujel Orhan Teachers' College, named for Halide's late father, consisted of three single-story, earth-brown buildings, each more than fifty meters in length, situated on a broad field overlooking the Bosphorous. The center structure appeared to be finished. The other two were half-completed, their roofs open to the elements. Halide greeted him at the front door, dressed in slacks and a heavy woolen sweater. Her hair was cut very short. He noticed she was starting to go gray at the temples.

Halide smiled broadly. "*Hosh geldiniz*! Welcome my friend. Although I don't know if I'd call someone who's known about this place for months and hasn't even visited 'a friend,'" she joked. "Even Lieutenant Colonel Akdemir graced me with his presence a few weeks ago. Now that you've finally arrived, allow me to give you the grand tour."

Halide wore a carpenter's belt, from which a number of tools were suspended. She walked with a determined gait that reminded him of the girl who'd fought her way through every obstacle to come to Gelibolu over seventeen years ago. Allah, they'd both been children back then. Down the hall, he heard the pounding of hammers, and good-natured, purposeful shouting. The noise was magnified because there was no carpeting to muffle its sound.

They entered a large room, where Turhan saw six burly fellows putting up large sheets of wallboard. The bright lighting stood in stark contrast to the gray outdoors. In an adjacent office, four young women were busily engaged sewing drapes and wall hangings. They looked up, nodded in greeting, and smiled as Halide introduced them to Turhan. While they were cordial, they were not about to be deterred from their work.

"It's not much to look at, yet," Halide shouted over the din. "But give it a year or so and you'll see something really special."

Farther down the hall, there were four classrooms and, beyond that, a men's dormitory and a women's dormitory, each containing twenty iron cots, an equal number of portable wooden closets, nightstands, chairs and desks. There were communal washrooms at the far end of each dormitory. "We've got thirty-four students and six teachers," Halide said proudly. "Twenty men, twenty women. All of the men, students and teachers, sleep in one bedroom, all the women in the other. We eat together, we study together, and we're building together."

"And if we don't work together a little harder, Hanım Effendim, we'll never be able to house the fifty additional students and eight new teachers who're supposed to be here in September." The strong, bass voice belonged to a tall, ruddy-complexioned man in his mid-twenties. "You must be Turhan Türkoğlu," the young man said, smiling and holding out his hand, western style.

Turhan shook it, impressed. "I'm afraid we haven't met."

"I'm Nurettin Shihan. I feel I've known you for months. Sezer's made me listen to 'The Voice of Turkey' every night. I wouldn't be surprised if every Turk within sound of your voice feels you're a member of his family."

"Thank you," Turhan said.

"This brash young fellow seems to think he owns the place," Halide said, smiling up at the large man. "I found him just before we started building," she continued. "Much as I'd like to believe Mustafa Kemal's posturing about how all men and women are created equal, anyone who believes that would as soon build a bridge over the Bosphorous. I simply couldn't function without Nurettin. He's the best contractor, negotiator, and administrator I've ever known. And to think I found him in my very own back yard. Praise Allah for our wonderful American friends who sent him over here from Robert College."

"Turhan Effendim, I'd love to stay and talk to you," Nurettin said, "but I've got work to do in the next building. We're trying to make it rival the Pera Palas," he said, grinning.

"But it's freezing out there," Turhan said.

"A little cold never hurt anyone. You don't sweat as much on a day like today." Three other men, of similar size and build, wearing sweaters, heavy coats, gloves and hats, joined him. After brief introductions, the work party departed.

Turhan followed Halide to her office, which was small but elegant. "Have a seat while I fix us some tea," she said, as she turned on the Victrola, and selected a Mozart sonata. "The college is less than a year old," she continued, "but it's a beginning. Sezer and two others teach the beginners. I'm the professor and dean. That means I get to work eighteen hours a day instead of the normal twelve. Occasionally, we all go up to my house, which I rather pretentiously call Belgrade Palas, for a weekend. I always was a better cook than a carpenter," she chuckled, then turned serious. "Now, my dear Turhan, what brings you to my humble abode on such a beautiful, warm day, as if I didn't know?"

"Sezer's told you?"

"Of course. I congratulate you on a rare opportunity to advance your career, my friend. Even if your wife's not pleased."

"Kemal wants us both to go to Berlin."

"Does that mean that Sezer has no choice in the matter?" Halide's tone was not challenging. If she was disturbed, she gave no sign of it.

"This is something more important than either of us. How can I turn down the Gazi?"

"You'd sacrifice your wife's happiness for your own career?"

"I don't follow you," he said.

"Why must she go?"

"It's an opportunity for both of us, far beyond anything ever offered before."

"It's an opportunity for *you*, my friend." She gazed at him steadily, her elbows spread on her desk, her hands cupping her chin. "What makes you think it would be an opportunity for Sezer?"

"Sezer's a village girl from Suvarli. Five years ago, she'd never have hoped to travel beyond her village, let alone go to a major European capital. How can she not see this is a dream come true?"

"It may be *your* dream, my friend. That doesn't mean it's hers."

"But I'm her husband!" he spluttered, exasperated at Halide's studied calm.

Now she raised her voice, ever so slightly. "Turhan, I'm surprised at you. We've known each other nearly eighteen years. Whatever happened to the caring friend who held my hand when Metin died? Have you become such a slave to your own ambition that you'd say such a thing? Is what you're doing any more important than Sezer's work?"

"You don't understand," he rejoined. "No woman could."

"I see." She colored. "Is that because we mere women don't possess your keen intelligence? Or have you fallen victim to the old saying, 'No one is so blind as he who will not see?'"

"You can't see my point at all."

"That's rather a cheap way of avoiding a direct answer."

He'd gotten no further with his dearest friend than he had with his wife.

"Is there no solution, then?"

"I don't know, Turhan," she said. "Sezer's torn between conflicting choices. She loves her work here. She honestly feels she is making a difference and she's right. She's miserable at the thought of betraying you, and she's frightened to death by what she's heard of Germany. You're right when you say perhaps we women don't entirely understand. After all, it's a man who's in power there. The things we read in newspapers and hear on the radio don't give us 'mere women' great comfort."

"Where is Sezer?" Turhan asked.

"I sent her to Bebek to try and sort out her thoughts. She said it would be too difficult to confront you in her present state. What about your thoughts?"

"The Gazi promised me a maximum of a year. Could the college survive her loss for that period?"

Halide opened her desk drawer, drew out a piece of paper and a pencil, and marked figures on the paper. "At present, we have thirty-four students and six teachers. How soon does Kemal want you there?"

"Two weeks from now. The beginning of February," Turhan said.

"Spring is our recruiting time. Normally, I'd have Sezer traverse the country, looking for likely candidates. We've already got a full complement for next year. Robert College can loan me a teacher to take Sezer's place. I don't see that as the significant problem."

"Well, then, it's settled. You should be able to convince her to go."

"Turhan, you listen but you don't hear. Why should I impose your will on another human being?"

"But you just said it wouldn't be a problem for you."

"What do you know about Germany, Turhan?"

"You mean about the Nazis?"

"No. The German character."

"What's to know?"

"I was raised in France. We were taught to mistrust the Germans. I'm sure they were taught that we French were a perfidious race. Still, both the Germans and French are *Western* Europeans. *Christian*, western Europeans, who look on Turks as Muslim scum, the defilers of babies, the murderers of millions of *Christian* Armenians. Add to that a very unique German character trait. They believe themselves to be the sons and daughters of the gods. It lives in everything they do. Do you know their national anthem?"

"*Deutschland, Deutschland über alles.*"

"Yes. Germany over all, over *everyone*. That's how they feel. They're not sorry about the last war. *They're sorry they lost it.* They've spent the last ten years searching for the betrayers in their midst. The politicians who signed the shameful Versailles Treaty, those who caused inflation to escalate until their proud nation was bankrupt. The one thing their character would never allow them to admit is that they were somehow at fault. It couldn't be Germans. They were too perfect. It had to be someone else."

"We were Germany's ally in the last war."

"And so were Germany's Jews, who gave their blood, their energy and their money," Halide continued. "But the Jews were part of a losing effort and the Turks were part of a losing effort. The very presence of non-Aryan outsiders inside their holy borders serves as a constant reminder that Germany was humiliated by children of a lesser god. Sezer's frightened. She has a right to be. If I were in her position, I'd resist too."

"But I'd be under the Gazi's protection," Turhan sputtered.

"How effective do you think that would be? Do you think the president would truly go to war over one Turk?"

"Are you saying we shouldn't go?"

"I'm not saying anything," Halide said. "The decision is not mine to make. There are other considerations. Turkish men have always been drawn to Germany like moths to a candle. I'm told Berlin is a decadent city, and there are sophisticated attractions to snare and hold any man. Certainly you're not a bloodless saint."

"Perhaps that's a reason she should accompany me. To protect her territory."

Halide scowled. "Is that the depth of your feeling for your wife, Turhan? That another human being is someone's possession, someone's 'territory?' Perhaps there are some important lessons you've yet to learn, my friend."

"I can see I'm getting nowhere," he responded. "I thought you'd be more help to me."

"Perhaps I am. Think about what I've said, Turhan. Maybe it's time you determined what your priorities were."

Turhan left a short while later. It was a tense parting for the two friends.

In the end, the matter was never quite resolved. Turhan Türkoğlu, the self-styled "Voice of Turkey," delivered his last broadcast from Radio House in Ankara on February 18, 1933. The following day, he left the Turkish capital to serve as Kemal's eyes and ears in the German capital. Despite her doubts and fears, Sezer accompanied her husband to the heart of the Third Reich. Not happily. Although they never said anything to one another about it, there was a polite unease between them. For it was clear that they had very different ideas about how best to serve their country.

8

When Kerem, his mentor, died in 1928, Abbas was relieved and secretly jubilant. The old man had become crippled with arthritis, then senile. The younger man continued to take care of him, insisting that the Brotherhood's weekly meetings be held in Kerem's home because of the elder's inability to travel. During the last five years, the man who'd lifted Abbas from the gutters of the bazaar had become an increasingly unbearable burden. He was incontinent much of the time. Abbas gagged at the foul odors that emanated from him. Sexual congress between them had ceased years ago, and Abbas had taken on a lover, a young army lieutenant who'd been inducted into the Brotherhood several months before.

Abbas was pleased, but not surprised, that he'd been appointed the old man's executor, and that Kerem had left him the bulk of his estate. After all, it had been Abbas who'd befriended the shady *avukat* and secured proper witnesses to Kerem's will. By that time, the old man could not see well enough to read and was lucid barely half the time. When Kerem's family protested the five percent of the estate they'd been left, the witnesses swore by Allah that the testator had been fully competent, indeed eager, to leave everything to his protégé, and that it had only been at Abbas' insistence that the family had gotten anything at all.

Now that Kerem was gone, Abbas suggested the Brotherhood meet at various locations. If it was to remain a *secret* organization, it would hardly do for prying eyes to wonder why thirty men congregated at the same place each Wednesday evening. "One could hardly imagine so many men came together to play *tavla*," he joked.

Abbas had secured regular promotions in the police department. At thirty-five, he was a captain. It was hinted that his promotions had come because of his extraordinary ability to ferret out crimes committed by those in positions of wealth and power, and because police coffers always swelled after an arrest by Hükümdar's units. Oddly, even though few of those arrested by Abbas were convicted, he gained a reputation as one of the toughest, most dedicated officers on the force. A few officers under him hinted that he was a sadistic bastard. When word reached him, these officers found themselves transferred to details so demeaning that shortly afterward they left the force.

One evening, half a year after Kerem's death, the host of that evening's Brotherhood meeting asked Abbas to stay on after the rest left. The young captain was flattered. The man was the third highest ranking officer in the Interior Ministry. At his invitation, Abbas joined the deputy in his private study.

"Cognac?" the older man, Zihat Ölmay, offered.

"Thank you, yes."

"Good. I appreciate a man who has cultured tastes. Captain Hükümdar, I asked you to stay because I've been impressed by your achievements."

"I didn't know you've been following them, Sir."

"You're a policeman. Your job is to know everything in your district. Mine is to know what's going on throughout the nation. We learn many things about all sorts of people."

Abbas sipped his brandy slowly. He'd learned when an older person was in an expansive mood, it was best to listen. The deputy continued. "Let me be frank with you, Abbas. You're a captain in the police force and you are ambitious are you not?"

"Yes, Sir."

"No one minds a dalliance here and there. Don't be surprised. I know about the lieutenant and I've known about Kerem for a long time. Men of the world don't bandy such things about. But if you're thinking about rising to the highest echelons, it becomes necessary to have the proper, ahem, trappings."

"What do you mean, Mister Minister?" Abbas said, elevating the man a couple of notches in rank.

"A wife to attend social functions. A child, perhaps two, to complete the family picture."

"Why would this be of concern to you, Sir?"

"Abbas, a father wants the best for his children. My daughter Mina is thirty-three and unmarried. She's not unattractive. I don't believe she'll ever set the world afire intellectually..."

"Are you suggesting an arranged marriage, Mister Minister?"

"There are worse things, Captain. There would be advantages to each side, of course."

"Of course."

"I'm not a pauper by any means, although I understand you've succeeded to an adequate estate of your own. There would be other benefits as well. I suggest you consider a lateral transfer from Internal Security Police to the Interior Ministry. Should you desire to exercise your – other needs – I trust you'd use discretion. There'd be ample opportunity for travel throughout Turkey and beyond."

Abbas mulled the suggestion over in his mind. The advantages far outweighed the disadvantages. Lately, his lover, the lieutenant had become tiresomely demanding. A son to carry on his name would not be a bad idea. Besides, a woman was only a vessel to bear his seed anyway. Did it matter who or how? He thought back to something a friend in the Brotherhood had told him once., "Your eyes are closed when you do it. You can imagine your partner to be whomever you choose."

"Mister Minister, this comes as a surprise, albeit not an unpleasant one. I'll need some time to digest it. May I respond to your proposal within the week?"

"Certainly."

His father-in-law was right. Mina was neither a fount of intelligence, nor an exciting or accomplished lover. But within a year of the marriage, Abbas had moved several rungs up the ladder in the Interior Ministry. In May, 1930, his wife gave birth to a son. Abbas became the brightest new star in the galaxy of deputy secretaries in the Interior Ministry.

"I think it's time to expand your horizons a bit."

"What do you mean, Papa?" Deputy Minister Ölmay enjoyed when his son-in-law professed familial feelings. Even though his daughter was no great prize, the younger man had more than made good on his promise and Abbas harbored genuine affection for him.

"One of the best ways to enhance professionalism is to observe and emulate those who do it better than anyone else. I admire the strategies employed by the National Socialists in Germany. Their entire philosophy is to purify the race. Germany for Germans."

Abbas grinned broadly. "Hasn't that been the Brotherhood's goal since its inception? To rid our own land of foreign elements?"

"Indeed." Ölmay smiled knowingly at the younger man. "The new German Chancellor surrounds himself with good men. Hitler's well aware that he who rules by fear is most in control. He's clever enough to use the Stürmabteilung to soften up his enemies while he plans greater long-range goals. There's talk he's planning to replace Department IA of the Prussian Political Police."

"So I've heard. You think he might be ready to dump Roehm?"

"Not yet, Abbas. After all, Roehm's one of his inner circle of five."

"But Hitler felt abandoned in 1925 when Roehm went to Bolivia as a lieutenant colonel."

"You've done your homework. Roehm's earned his way back into the Führer's good graces. The S.A., the National Socialists' private militia, was out of hand when Hitler asked him to come back and take over. But we're not here to discuss German politics. This is the *Turkish* Interior Ministry. I'd like you to go to Germany – unofficially, of course – and meet with a few of my acquaintances. Find out what they're up to."

"How long would I be there?"

"A few months."

"Would Mina and the boy be going with me?"

"I think not. She's pregnant again. Your son's two – a horrible age, is it not? We'll be pleased to take care of them. I've heard Berlin is a *very* cosmopolitan city, one that could be a great deal of fun. No need to take a day-old sandwich to a banquet, eh?" He winked conspiratorially.

"Who am I supposed to see?"

"Two men in particular. Heinrich Himmler, who's a real manipulator, and a fellow more your own age who I think you'll enjoy immensely, Reinhard Heydrich. Never mind the arrogant Aryan face he shows the world. He'll show you a very good time."

9

Turhan and Sezer flew from Istanbul to Bucharest, thence directly to Berlin on the *Deutsche Lufthansa* international flight. When they arrived at Tempelhof, they were struck by the efficiency and spotless cleanliness of the *flughafen,* and by a large cadre of brown-shirted toughs, ostensibly "keeping order," who appeared to be roughing up several older people.

"S.A., Hitler's private militia," Turhan whispered to Sezer. "I expect before long, we'll see several more of these brown-shirt toughs."

They were met by the Turkish ambassador, who showed them to their apartment in the Münchenerstrasse. "On President Kemal's orders, the Turkish government will provide your apartment. You have direct contact by telephone with the embassy. If you need anything, day or night," he said, handing Turhan a small piece of paper, "telephone this number and identify yourself."

"Thank you, Your Excellency. I'm surprised. I was told I was not an official with the embassy."

"You're not." He dropped the formality and smiled. "Let's say the *Gazi* would be most upset if he thought any harm could come to you. Oh, by the way, Turhan Effendim?"

"Yes?"

"Would you mind terribly signing your autograph – for my wife, of course. We always listened to you on Radio Ankara."

"It would be my pleasure, Excellency."

"*Chok teshekkür ederim*, many thanks. We're having a grand party to celebrate *Sheker Bayram* in six days, on February 27, at the embassy. Herr Hitler sent his regrets, but we expect a most pleasant gathering of our international community. I'd feel honored if you and your wife could attend. It would give you a fine introduction to life in Berlin."

Even before sunset, replicas of ancient Turkish lanterns lit the half-circular driveway in front of the embassy. As Mercedes, Bugattis, and Daimlers arrived, white haired, bewhiskered doormen, outfitted in flowing robes and turbans, presented each alighting passenger with a souvenir of Turkey, a hand carved meerschaum pipe for each man, a single rose in a small alabaster vase for his lady. Formally dressed guests murmured appreciatively as they were escorted over the finest *Hereke*, *Bünyan* and *Kayseri* carpets, into the cavernous ballroom. A white canvas tent, extending from floor to ceiling, draped the entire room. A huge ball, with hundreds of mirrored glass squares embedded in its surface, hung from the ceiling. Spotlights on either side of the room were aimed at the ball. As the huge fixture rotated, a thousand bursts of light created an ever-changing kaleidoscope of artificial stars.

Three hundred guests sat on low cushions, placed atop an even greater array of Turkish carpets than they'd seen at the door. They were treated to a scene befitting a deliciously scandalous and decadent land of sultans and harems. Veiled women in diaphanous gowns, with long, black hair wafted by the low tables, leaving behind a mild scent of incense and spices. In each corner of the room a fierce looking Turk, his head shaved, his mammoth chest bared, removed a razor-sharp scimitar from a sash tied around his midriff, and commenced slicing meat that was roasting on a vertical, rotating spit. The veiled women approached each of the monstrous Turks, carrying large dinner plates, covered with flat bread. The swordsmen placed generous portions of the meat on the plates, after which the women returned, serving each guest.

At each table, there were *jezves*, small, long-handled brass pots with pouring spouts, filled with freshly melted garlic-butter, or an aromatic sauce of mushrooms, tomatoes, eggplant, onion and garlic to pour over the meat.

The women served heaping bowls of rice, crisp, fresh salads, and bottles of *Chankaya*, a light, delicate white wine, and *Doluja*, a full bodied red, both varieties grown, harvested and bottled in Turkey.

"By Jove, you Turks must lead a splendid life under President Kemal," a florid-faced, monocled Englishman said to Turhan.

"You'd think so to look at this," Turhan muttered. "The average Turk never lived like this. Even the wealthiest haven't seen such splendor in the past hundred years."

"Yes, but this is Berlin. A little show never hurt anyone, eh?"

"I disagree. The whole world is in the middle of the worst depression in the past half-century. The money spent to entertain these overfed dilettantes could feed and house three thousand Turks for a year! The Gazi would not tolerate this display for a moment."

"The Huns seem to be putting on their own show now that Adolf is in power," the Englishman said.

"Another diversion. Keep the masses busy. Give them circuses so they won't know there's no bread."

"Well, er, yes. Excuse me, if you will. I didn't catch your name. I'm sure I shall as the night progresses." The man departed.

"My husband makes his debut as society's most brilliant light," Sezer remarked.

"People like him will be the first to cave in when Hitler starts making demands."

"What do you mean, darling?"

"What I see going on, even in the few days I've been here, distresses me greatly. The diplomats toady up to the Führer as though he's the next Caesar. Beneath it all, there's an undercurrent of fear. In Turkey, everyone speaks his mind, sometimes too much so. Here, in this 'civilized' land, I sense terror just below the glittering surface. People are so cautious when they speak."

"You're absolutely right, Türkoğlu," an American-accented voice behind him said. "In medieval times, they say scholars argued for hours about how many angels could dance on the head of a pin. These fools are those very angels, dancing on the edge of the abyss. It's amazing that so few of them see that."

Turhan turned and found himself looking into the clear, brown eyes of a man in his thirties, with thinning hair and thick spectacles. The man smiled and pumped Turhan's hand. "I'm Ed Baumueller, New York *World*. I happened to be in Berlin and your ambassador kindly invited me to fill a vacant space."

"Mr. Baumueller – of *the* Baumuellers? The ones who founded the *World*?"

"Don't tell anyone," he said in a stage whisper. "We're a Jewish-owned outfit. That wouldn't go down well with His Holiness, the next Frederick Barbarossa."

As the two men became involved in the camaraderie shared by newspapermen everywhere, the ambassador's wife drew Sezer into a circle of Turkish women. Turhan and Baumueller had been talking for five minutes when a man approached and greeted the American in heavily accented English. "Herr Baumueller, I was asked by an old friend, Paul Gottlober, to convey his greetings."

"Gottlober? His father and mine went to school together, many years ago. You seem awfully young to be one of his associates."

"He gave me my first job in sales. I am Bernhard Friedman. Ten years ago, I traveled to New York and observed how Jews have done so well in your country. Macy, Gimbel, Levi Strauss, and, of course, your own family."

"What do you do, Herr Friedman?"

"I took a lesson from your American Jews. I started my own dry goods store. I was lucky – the Yiddish word is 'Mazeldicke' – and it prospered. Then I built another, and another. So now I am fortunate that the name 'Friedman' is known from Berlin to Vienna."

"Friedman's Department Store. Of course!" Turhan said, brightening. "I saw the three-story building in Unter den Linden. That was the first place the ambassador's wife took us to shop."

"You must be Turhan Türkoğlu, the newspaper journalist and radio personality."

"I'm flattered you would know such things."

"Herr Türkoğlu, I'm a merchant. It's my job to know every potential customer." He laughed easily. "Seriously, the ambassador told me you'd arrived. He gave me instructions to treat you with great courtesy. It seems you have friends in very high places in the Turkish Republic."

After a few minutes of pleasantries, Turhan asked, "Mr. Friedman, can you give me your candid opinion about what will happen to the Jews with the Führer in power?"

"Of course. I believe his anti-Jewish talk will blow over. Storm clouds have always hovered over the house of Israel. We Jews have kept the mercantile life of Germany going since the Middle Ages. Where would the universities, the law courts, the great orchestras be without us? The Führer may rant and rave about *Juden* this and *Juden* that, and how Jews have polluted the master race. That's nothing more than a device to obtain votes. Why, I've donated several thousand *Reichshmarks* to his campaign – as I have to the campaigns of all the major candidates. In the end, I've always found these politicians know where their bread is buttered and who pays for their tirades."

"You don't think all this anti-Semitic talk will last?" Baumueller asked.

"Hardly," Friedman responded. "The brown shirts will carry on for a while. The *Reichskanzler* may let them throw a few stones or tease our poorer *landsmen*. Give Hitler a couple years to consolidate his power and he'll be like all the rest. Fat, content with what he has, squirreling away as much as he can in a numbered Swiss bank account for the day he leaves office."

"My husband talks a brave game. I'm not sure I agree. I believe Hitler is a dangerous madman. Anyone who attempts to predict what he'll do is a fool." Turhan found himself staring into the largest, deepest eyes he'd ever seen, green with pale yellow flecks. The woman's oval-shaped, freckled face was framed by shoulder-length auburn hair. Turhan felt an electric shock, followed by a fleeting wave of guilt as he glanced over to where Sezer had been standing a few moments ago.

"Gentlemen, I don't know how outspoken women are in your countries, but it's certainly not Jewish tradition to silence our wives. Rachela, may I introduce you to Herr Edwin Baumueller of the New York *World* and Herr Turhan Türkoğlu of the Turkish radio and the newspaper Isharet."

"I'm pleased to meet you both." Her voice was warm. She was barely five feet tall, slender, and most attractive. She came up to Turhan's shoulders. She wore a black sheath gown that accentuated her slight, but definite, feminine curves. Rachela Friedman wore no scent. Turhan noticed a clean, light aroma when he stood near her. He wondered what she looked like beneath the dress. Would her whole body be as freckled as her face? He felt a hot flush suffuse his neck. The woman appeared not to notice.

"Do you find Berlin much different from Ankara, Herr Türkoğlu?" she asked.

"It's a little early to make a judgment, Frau Friedman," he replied. His voice sounded natural, despite the trip-hammer pounding he felt in his chest. "I'm impressed by your neatly kept, green parks and your shops filled with so many things we don't have in Turkey."

"Yes," she murmured. "The Germans have always been very meticulous. They work together like cogs in a well-oiled machine. Why shouldn't they? They are the sons and daughters of the gods."

Turhan said nothing. He was dumbfounded. Halide had spoken those precise words less than a month before. Rachela Friedman continued, "They give minute attention to detail. Every rose in our municipal gardens must be perfect. Every tree must be just so. They say the Führer wishes to purify the German race along the same lines."

"What do you think of all this, Frau Friedman? You appear to be an informed German citizen."

"You are wrong, Mister Türkoğlu. I'm a *Jewish* German citizen. That makes a rather significant difference."

"Darling, sshhh," her husband interjected. "You never know who might be listening."

She continued, caustically mimicking her husband. "Sssh. You never know who might be listening. It doesn't matter who hears, Bernhard. We are doomed if we stay in Germany. And it won't only be us. There are gypsies and Catholics, communists, Slavs, Turks for that matter..."

Turhan looked directly at this beautiful, sophisticated woman.

"You heard me correctly, Mister Türkoğlu. Turks, Russians, Frenchmen, it doesn't really matter. Have you ever been an outsider, Mister Türkoğlu? I mean a *real* outsider? Do you have any sense of what it means to be an outcast simply because of an accident of birth? Have you ever known what it is to be completely helpless? To foresee your future in a cracked mirror, knowing you are tied to that future because you haven't the courage to make the right decision?"

He looked deeply into the woman's green, yellow-flecked eyes, and saw something there he didn't want to see. A combination of danger, vivacity and hopelessness that touched the core of his soul. This was neither a spoiled child-woman nor a brittle socialite. This one understood, and saw the future. This one knew.

At that moment, Turhan was assaulted by a series of uncomfortable and conflicting feelings. Unquestionably he felt a bold stab of lust for this beautiful woman, who was a world apart from his own Sezer – a world apart even from someone as attractive and sophisticated as Aysheh Akdemir. But there was more to his feelings than that. He saw a deeply troubled future for the tiny woman. He wanted to hold her, to comfort her, to assure her that everything would be all right. But he was deeply uncertain if things *would* work out for this Jewess, who was as much an outsider as he had felt himself to be in his youth. Turhan was troubled. Deeply troubled.

A few nights later, Turhan and Sezer received an invitation to dine at the Friedmans. The Turkish ambassador provided an embassy limousine and chauffeur for the evening. When they arrived at the elegant estate, they were surprised to see a pair of uniformed officers wearing Swastika arm bands, standing just outside the electric gate.

"It's a good thing we don't have a car of our own," Turhan remarked, feeling the guards' sinister look. "I'm certain they'd have marked our arrival."

"Don't be too sure they haven't," Sezer remarked uneasily.

Once inside the gates, there was no hint of anything amiss. The large Mercedes crunched over the circular driveway. As they stopped in front of the entryway to the two-story, classic structure with its pseudo-Greek columns, a footman promptly opened the limousine's door. Turhan did not miss the tiny red, white and black Nazi flag pinned to the footman's lapel.

As Turhan and Sezer entered the heavy oak double doors, they found themselves in a rich, tastefully furnished hallway. A butler led them directly to the formal dining room, where a teakwood table was set with Bohemian crystal, English bone china, and German silverware, all in the best of taste. A crystal chandelier, which matched the glassware, hung suspended from a high, marbled ceiling.

"Good evening Herr und Frau Türkoğlu. I'm so pleased you could come on such short notice." Bernhard Friedman was dressed in an elegant, black tuxedo with maroon bow tie and matching cummerbund.

"It is indeed our pleasure," Turhan answered, nodding his head formally. "In fact, it's our first invitation other than the 'command performance' at the embassy the other night."

"My wife will be down momentarily," Friedman continued. "Since the night of the Reichstag fire, the Führer's decided to post sentries about the homes of Berlin's wealthier Jews. Rachela's quite nervous about it, although I've tried to convince her it's simply another ploy to show the extent of the Reich Chancellor's control."

"I can well understand her fear, Herr Friedman," Sezer said. "The specter of such guards frightens me as well."

"As I'm certain it's meant to do, Frau Türkoğlu. The display of power has always been a German characteristic."

"And we women are expected to sit by and watch as our brave men play their cat-and-mouse games." Rachela Friedman entered the room, looking exquisite in a pale peach evening gown. Her words jarred Turhan as he recalled another night in a village in Anatolia so many years ago. The night the Turks decided to show the Armenians who was in power.

"Enough of such matters," their host said genially. "We've invited our newest friends for a pleasant social evening, and I refuse to spoil it just because a couple of ruffians want to brave the chill night air outside our gates." The servant who'd greeted them in the entry hall, held out the ladies' chairs. He was a dignified old man, bewhiskered in the courtly manner of the old Germany.

"Ludwig's been a family retainer for... how long?" Bernhard asked, glancing up.

"Forty-one years, Herr Friedman. Before that, I served your father, Sir."

"Tell me, Ludwig," their host said expansively. "What do you think of all this National Socialist buildup?"

"I'm not political, Sir. I'm surprised that von Hindenburg seems to have entered into an alliance with them."

"The old man's mostly senile, Ludwig."

"Still, Herr Friedman, he does have a following in Germany."

"There, Bernhard," Rachela interrupted. "Does that show you that these people are serious?" Her smile was bleak. Turhan felt the tension in the room.

"Achh, it's nothing," her husband said. "A consolidation of his power, nothing more."

The servant turned and discreetly left the room. Immediately Rachela became more composed. "I'm sorry if I've upset you both," she said, turning her gaze to Turhan. "But I felt that you, as a reporter, should try to get an objective view of what's going on so you might let others know."

"Herr Friedman," Turhan spoke up. "I don't say I doubt your word, but just in case there's some validity to what your wife says, have you arranged for any options?"

"There's no need for them," the merchant said smoothly. "Even should the Chancellor extend his Jew-baiting games, the German people would never go along with it. They know that we're as loyal as they to the fatherland and that the loss of the merchant class would cripple their already weak economy."

"But what if things truly did get worse? Could you envision a time when Hitler might close the borders?"

Rachela was looking directly at him. He felt an alliance between them, but more than that, he felt a renewal of the lightning jolt he'd felt the night of the Embassy party. Her eyes were dazzling, but it was her presence that moved him most.

"Close the borders, Türkoğlu? I should think he'd open them and help them be on their way if he truly wanted to dispose of Jews," Friedman said.

"Would you leave the Reich, darling?" Rachela asked. "You have several department stores. How easily could you give up the stores, this estate, our naïvely spoiled way of life?"

Friedman sat in silence for awhile, chewing a bit of the perfectly prepared roast brisket. He did not seem the least upset by his wife's outburst. When he spoke, his tone was quiet, thoughtful. "I would think it very hard to leave such a life, Rachela. Praise God it will never happen during our lifetimes."

"Herr Friedman," Sezer said. "I don't mean to be impolite, but it seems you don't want to be burdened with these questions. Women have a stronger intuition than you might realize. I share your wife's concern. Nothing good can come of this."

"That's not necessarily so, Frau Türkoğlu. Our unemployment lines shrink each day. There's food in circulation, and some money. Even I have to admit that things seem better now than they did a few months ago. There's a sense of dedication I've not experienced before."

"Ah, but dedication to what, Herr Friedman?" Turhan asked. "And at whose expense? It seems this economy is fueled on terror, on compliant silence. I'm not saying Turkey's a great beacon of enlightenment, but we're free to say what we please, and most Turks certainly do just that. There is a strong Jewish community in Istanbul that's been there for hundreds of years. You should consider visiting our country. There's no telling when you might need a safe harbor, and Turkey could well provide it."

For the first time that evening, Rachela's eyes took on a hopeful light. She gazed at Turhan in frank appreciation. The room suddenly felt very warm.

"Perhaps one day we shall do just that, Herr Türkoğlu," Friedman said. "But for the present, we are too taken up with our businesses. We've just introduced the spring line, and in another month it'll be time to consider our autumn selection of ladies' clothes."

After dinner, Bernhard invited his guests to sit on the veranda and enjoy a bracing Berlin spring evening. They'd been outside a quarter of an hour when the sky clouded over. A swift thunderstorm drove them inside, but within the hour it had cleared and a bright crescent moon appeared. "A good omen, my friends," Bernhard remarked. "Just as the storm has passed us by leaving the beautiful silver light of the moon, so will the problems we discussed earlier pass as well."

"I would hope so," Turhan murmured. "But I've learned over the years that to stay aware is to stay alive."

"The Friedman woman's very beautiful, isn't she?" Sezer said as they were preparing for bed.

"Perhaps, but she couldn't hold a candle to you, darling," he said dutifully, although his thoughts hadn't left Rachela for a moment since they'd left the Friedman's sumptuous home. "You know," he said, changing the subject, "I'm beginning to think you might have been right. Perhaps this is not the time to be in Berlin."

She smiled at him and squeezed his hand. When Turhan looked at Sezer's lovely, placid face, he saw trust and innocence there. This was his wife, his helpmate, a woman who'd traveled a thousand miles to be by his side. His comfort and support. Still, he felt disquieted, disturbed. And only he knew why.

Their lovemaking that night was tender, satisfying. Turhan vowed he'd remain faithful to their marriage bed, thankful that Allah had given him a signal to return with a full heart to the safety and security of his chosen mate. But as Sezer moaned with passion, he saw another face, experienced another body. When it was over, he lay wide awake while his wife slept peacefully. His thoughts never left Rachela. For no reason he could ever hope to explain, he felt an incredible bond with her, unlike anything he'd ever felt before. And he trembled.

10

March 8, 1933, Berlin
Personal and confidential
VIA DIPLOMATIC POUCH

My Gazi:

You asked me to be your eyes and ears in this place for a year, but you gave me leave to write articles for Isharet *describing my feeling about what I see. I ask your permission to express those opinions truthfully. I fear if I do so, I will not last out the year in this place.*

The Germans were our allies in the Great War, but the Germany we knew is no more, perhaps because the peace treaty imposed upon Germany was so cruel it enabled Hitler to come to power. Or perhaps it is something deep within the German character.

The aftermath of the Reichstag fire was bizarre. Hindenburg signed an emergency decree that cancelled every personal liberty. The government now has the legal right to open all telegrams and letters, and to intercept telephone communications. Hitler's National Socialist Party, which calls itself the government, can confiscate property at will. It's hard to believe the "civilized" Germans accepted it. Police can arrest anyone and extend the period of detention indefinitely. They can deny an arrestee the right to see a lawyer. They don't even have to tell his relatives anything about the reason for the arrest, or the fate of the person arrested. These arbitrary abuses never get into the court record.

The German people walk about in a daze. Ten thousand have been arrested in Prussia since the indefinite "emergency" decree. On the eve of the March 5 election, I was in Königsberg and witnessed one of Hitler's grand theatrical shows. A hundred thousand people attended. At the end of his speech, church bells pealed all over the city. The man is a spellbinder, but no good can come of his policies.

The Nazi dreamers expected to gain nearly a hundred percent of the vote in the March 5 election. Between Hitler's inflammatory rhetoric and the intense pressures put on the man in the street, how could anyone vote otherwise and live to tell about it? Yet, the National Socialists only got forty-four percent of the popular vote, and had to rely on Hindenburg to form a coalition government. Even then, their majority was less than fifty-two percent. Yesterday, in the strange alchemy that allows Hitler to spin gold from straw, the chancellor proclaimed the election had been a "revolution," and ordered the Nazi flag, the Swastika, run up on all public buildings.

Gazi, I urge extraordinary caution in dealing with this "government." Hitler's henchmen are dangerous and unpredictable. Take care.

Sincerely, Turhan

In April, there was a spring thaw in the German capital. The linden trees burst into full bloom. The sun shown brightly through the windows of the Turkish ambassador's office. Although radiators kept the embassy fifteen degrees warmer than outdoors, the atmosphere in the room was chilly. "Doctor von Papen," the ambassador began, "I'm always pleased to speak with someone from the foreign ministry. You are welcome in my residence."

"Thank you, Mister Ambassador. The pleasure is mine. Unfortunately, I must be blunt with you."

"Is something amiss?"

"Mister Ambassador, you're aware of the, ahem, very special relationship that has always existed between the peoples of Turkey and Germany."

"Yes, of course."

"You know the Führer wants nothing to impede that precious affiliation."

Get on with it, man, the ambassador thought. Sometimes he got tired of Papen's constant, long-winded posturing. "Yes," he said.

"Herr Göebbels has been reading the foreign press of late. You are no doubt aware of the scandalous lies being spread about the Reich Chancellor?" The ambassador said nothing. Papen continued. "We expect, of course, that it is in the interests of the French and English to poison the world's opinion against us. The Reich is prepared to deal with enemy propaganda. We certainly do not expect such treatment from our loyal friends and allies."

"What do you mean?"

The minister extracted a series of neatly clipped articles. Each bore the by-line of Turhan Türkoğlu. "Read them for yourself."

The ambassador thumbed through the clippings. The headlines told the story. *"ON THE WAY TO A FÜHRER STATE!" "MINORITIES BEWARE, YOU COULD BE NEXT!" "GERMAN CONSTITUTION DIES BY THE FÜHRER'S HAND!"*

"Excellency, you've been to Turkey many times. You know we have a free press. What this man says does not necessarily reflect our government's views."

"But he's in Germany, under the protection of your embassy. Our people are well aware that Türkoğlu is Kemal's spy."

"Herr von Papen," the ambassador said stiffly, "Turhan Türkoğlu is accredited to the foreign press corps by your own government. He is a private – I repeat, a *private* – Turkish citizen. His views are his own. As a Turk, he is entitled to whatever protection our embassy can afford its nationals."

"You've not answered my question. Is he or is he not under your president's personal protection?"

"I have nothing official to say, Herr von Papen. Are you telling me your government wants us to muzzle him?"

"I'm only saying he'd better watch what he says."

A few nights later, Turhan and Sezer were walking home from the American Press Club. They'd enjoyed *Grand Hotel*, one of the few American films being shown in Germany these days. As they approached the intersection of Unter den Linden and Museumstrasse, they were attracted by a large crowd outside Friedman's Department Store. Fifty brown-shirted SA troops had cordoned off the area around the store. They bore signs that read *"Deutsche! Wehrt Gut! Kauft nicht bei Juden!"* Several other toughs were plastering garishly colored signs all over the front walls, printed in German, which exhorted, "Germans! Arm yourselves against Jewish atrocity propaganda! Buy only at German shops!" The doors to the department store were locked. Iron bars covered the windows. Half a dozen brown shirts smashed at the protective coverings with sledge hammers. Turhan shuddered. He recalled a burning church in a small village in southeastern Turkey.

"Turhan, I'm frightened. I want to go home."

"I agree, darling. It's only a few blocks from here."

"No, Turhan, I mean *home*. To Turkey. How much longer can we pretend we don't see what's going on? I refuse to have someone spit in my face and force me to say, 'It must be rain.'"

"I promised the *Gazi* we'd stay a year."

"You heard what the ambassador said about his visit from Papen. Do you think you'll survive a year in this place?"

"If people like me aren't around, there'll be no one to tell the truth. I've got to risk the danger."

"You may have to do it without me, then. Much as it is my duty to be by your side, I can't sit idly by and watch you risk your life every time you pick up your pen."

"Come, darling. You're distressed by what we've seen tonight. I'll speak to the ambassador tomorrow morning about greater precautions for us."

As they rounded the corner to their block, a black car pulled up beside them. Four huge men, armed with clubs, climbed out. "There's the Turk *scheissdreck!*" one of them snarled. They grabbed Turhan roughly and threw him to the ground. Sezer screamed. The sound was cut short as one of the men smacked her across the face. She fell to the ground, her mouth bleeding. While she lay moaning, the other three clubbed and kicked Turhan in his stomach, his ribs, his face, and the back of his neck. Turhan's eyes were tearing. Within a few minutes at most, they'd be swollen shut. "*Verkackte drecksau!*" he heard a rough voice. "Shitfaced pig! I'll teach you to insult the Führer, you barbarian Turk!"

"Enough, Horst!" another voice said. "Our orders were to teach him a lesson, not to kill him. His apartment's just up the street."

The four men stopped beating Turhan and Sezer and headed toward the reporter's residence.

Thursday, May 25, 1933
Personal and Confidential

My Dear Papa:

*You were absolutely right. Heydrich's showed me a **very** good time. I need not go into details. As you and I have often discussed, you're a man of the world and understand such things. Even I was surprised at how jaded some of the nightclubs are. You can get anything, and I mean **anything** here.*

In my last letter, I told you Roehm's brown shirt toughs are having a wonderful time at the expense of the Jews – something we might think about when we realize they still control our Covered Bazaar. A lot of hooliganism and head-bashing, but their actions are boring and common, without any finesse.

I think Hitler realizes this. A month ago, Göring established a replacement for Department IA. At first, he'd intended to designate it merely as the Geheimes Polizei Amt, *the Secret Police Office, but the German initials GPA resembled the Soviet GPU which has bad connotations here. Himmler told me a postal employee came up with the name **Geheime Staatspolizei**, the Secret State Police, GESTAPO for short. Göring seems to be using it to arrest and dispose of opponents of the regime.*

Heydrich tells me the real future of state security will rest not so much with the GESTAPO, but with a group within the SS he and Himmler are planning, the Sicherheitsdienst. *He thinks it'll take them a year or two at least to convince der Führer of the need for yet **another** police organization. I'm impressed that both these men view law enforcement both as a science **and** an art. We can learn from the sophistication of their methods.*

*Our own ambassador's quite two-faced. On the one hand, he enjoys being the social lion in the eyes of the foreign community. On the other, he's made no secret of his contempt for the German regime. I've made it a point to steer clear of him. The old buzzard'll get in trouble for his views one day, and you've advised me how important it is to keep all my options open. I wish he were more like the Führer's foreign minister, von Papen. Now **there's** a real diplomat, erudite, confident, not about to take any garbage from anyone.*

I look forward to coming home in the next month. I've seen what I want to see and the joys have been immense. But family and duty calls. Auf wiedersehen.

Abbas

The Turkish ambassador climbed the marble steps of the German Foreign Ministry in cold fury. As he opened the heavy door and walked down the high-ceilinged entry hall, he tried to calm himself. His outrage increased when the foreign minister left him cooling his heels in an outer office for nearly an hour.

"I must protest in the strongest terms imaginable," he said angrily to von Papen.

"A Turkish national, returning to his legal residence, supposedly under the protection of your police force and the Turkish government, was brutally savaged, his apartment vandalized. Every bit of furniture and clothing was thrown out into the street and burned. I demand your government bring these felons to justice immediately!"

"Mister Ambassador," the minister replied. "Calm yourself. The Reich is a sovereign state, made up of free German citizens who have the right to express their opinions, just as your Herr Türkoğlu has the right to express his. Occasionally, these things get out of hand. Are you certain Herr Türkoğlu did nothing to provoke what occurred?"

"Herr Reichminister," the ambassador said, barely concealing his disgust, "you say all the right words in diplomatically suave tones. You know as well as I that what you are saying is *kuhmist*! This was an unprovoked, scurrilous, vicious attack on innocent human beings. Rest assured Kemal has heard of it. I am here at his personal demand."

"Herr Bötschafter, please convey to your president that the Reich Chancellor will do whatever he can to protect any foreign visitor to *Deutschland*. Not even Kemal can expect more than that."

"Listen, you smooth-talking hypocrite, if it happens again..."

"Then what, Mr. Ambassador? You'll take your diplomatic mission home? Let's not forget who's paying the bill for your stay in our fair city. Or what proud, but very poor nation has, at this very moment, several thousand workers in our capital, sending home *reichsmarks* to keep your country afloat. You're not a stupid man, *Effendim*," the foreign minister spoke condescendingly. "You understand the way the real world works. I said we will do what we can to apprehend the men who allegedly attacked your libelous reporter. Do I need to make myself any clearer, *Herr Bötschafter*?"

The ambassador flushed scarlet, turned on his heel, and slammed the ministry door on his way out.

Less than two weeks later, a black-uniformed factotum arrived at the Turkish embassy and presented a letter bearing the official seal of the foreign ministry. When the ambassador opened it and read the cryptic words, his hands trembled.

"To the Turkish Ambassador, Greeting:

"During the past six months, we have watched the continued libel of the German nation by the Turkish national Turhan Türkoğlu. The Reichskanzler, speaking through the Minister of Information and Propaganda, has concluded that amicable relations between our two independent states ought not be embarrassed by small elements of unnecessary friction.

"Accordingly, the Reich Foreign Ministry, acting upon the order of Reichskanzler and Führer Adolf Hitler, declares Turhan Türkoğlu persona non grata within the Third Reich. All credentials issued to him are revoked forthwith. Herr Türkoğlu is expelled. You are requested to remove him from Germany within the next twenty-four hours."

When he was confronted with the curt order, Turhan could only murmur, "Allah be praised. We are free at last. Mister Ambassador, you must remain here. You have our deepest sympathies."

11

"Was it that bad, Turhan?"

"Gazi," Turhan said, addressing Mustafa Kemal, his friend and the undisputed leader of Turkey, "you'd have to be there to experience it. They've started shipping 'undesirables' to a new kind of institution, a 'concentration camp.'"

"That's not so new, Turhan. Our American friends sent their native tribes to what they termed 'territories.'"

"Kemal Effendim, these are not the same kinds of places."

"You weren't any more popular with the German government than they were with you. Did you ever think you might be a bit too outspoken for your own good?"

"Is that a veiled hint, Mr. President?"

"An observation."

"Do you believe truth to be a relative thing, Gazi?"

"Do you, Turhan?"

"No. I believe truth is an absolute."

"Truth, my friend, depends on the point from which you're viewing it. What do you plan to do now?"

"I thought I'd apply for my old job on the Ankara radio."

"Even if some of your subject matter was censored?"

"Such as?"

"Although you may not feel warmth toward the Third Reich, Turkey must walk a path of strictest neutrality. The radio is a government organ."

"What about what I write for *Isharet*?"

"I can't stop what Selimiye wants to print. Turkey has a free press."

"Allah be thanked."

Turhan became *Isharet's* Istanbul bureau chief. During the next two years, he printed two versions of every article he wrote. The first, written for *Isharet*, was fitting for a metropolitan daily journal of international repute. The second, for which he never received payment, was written in a much simpler style, and was distributed to Turkey's small villages, for inclusion in their news-papers. From time to time, several thousand people read his *Isharet* articles. But Turhan was proudest of the second group of stories which entertained, informed, and educated the fifteen million villagers, who spent time sounding out each word in a hundred word article, then reread the article a dozen times to their wives and children.

This was a time of vast change in Turkey. Turkish women were given the right to vote in national elections. In November, 1934, every Turk was required to adopt a surname. If there had been twenty Mehmets in a village, they might have been identified in the past as "Mehmet the short," "Mehmet the vain," "Mehmet the water-carrier," and so forth. Now, last names became formalized. Sons would carry their fathers' surnames forward into untold generations.

Within a moment of his decision, "Mehmet-the-Ugly" shed the despised name *chirkin*, and henceforth was known as Mehmet *Shanli*,

"Mehmet the Glorious." People chose names as widely scattered as the human mind could imagine. The only exception to unlimited choice was that no one could choose the name the *Gazi* conferred upon himself, *Atatürk*, Father Turk.

Turhan's articles appealed to the villagers' superstitions, prejudices, and their ribald sense of humor, for the journalist, whose name was known to more Turks than the president of the republic, had been a village boy himself. A typical Türkoğlu admonition was, "Beware, lest a man cavalierly pick the name '*Büyükkamish*,' to describe his nether parts, and disappointed women discover that his self-advertised size does not fulfill the promise." Turhan's subject matter was universal. One week he wrote about new, inexpensive medicines. Another time, he might give advice to lovelorn young people. If the spirit moved him, he would write out the lyrics of a popular song, so an aspiring vocalist could read, as well as hear, the words to the tune.

Turhan fulfilled his promise to bring the world to the Dorutays of Turkey. Through his articles, Turks became aware that a small, quiet woman had organized the Yujel Orhan Teachers' College on the shores of the Bosphorous, and that because of Halide's efforts, four hundred teachers now traversed every part of Anatolia, instructing everyone who wanted to learn, and recruiting trainees who would teach in years to come.

But Turhan's consuming passion was the spread of what he perceived as absolute truth. He detested what he had seen taking place in Germany. Yet, he was fascinated by the strange goings-on in that European nation, and the apparent reticence on the part of the western allies to do anything to stop the Führer. In a series of *Isharet* articles, Turhan warned his countrymen of the sinister growth of the Reich. He excoriated Germany for the "benefits" it had brought to Turkey over the years. He reminded Turks that the reason it took so long to go by train from Ankara to Istanbul was that Turkey's German friends had contracted to build the intercity railway on a "per kilometer" basis. The Germans had taken full advantage of the opportunity. The result was a serpentine line that meandered all over the country. He wrote, "We need not speak of how we were Germany's lackeys in the Great War, and how, when the end came, our good friends blew up their ammunition dumps, leaving Turkey totally unarmed. Of infinitely greater consequence is the superior technology that led our allies to construct Ankara's water system, with the sewer lines going out of the city directly on top of the water lines coming into the capital. As a result, Ankara's water has a foul brown look, a putrid smell, and is unsafe to drink."

It was not risky for Turhan to chide the government for selecting a capital city where water was so scarce each home was allotted one hour's running water during each twenty-four hour period. A day's supply had to be stored in rusting steel drums. Ankara's residents accepted this minor inconvenience in exchange for the privilege of being close to power. It was quite another thing for *Isharet's* reporter to take on the president's 'sacred cow,' *Etatism* – the involvement of the state in every facet of Turkish life.

By the end of summer, 1937, Turhan believed Kemal's five year plan for industrial development, which called for the state to run all of Turkey's basic industries, was a disaster. The program created wealth for a privileged few, sapped the country's energy, and created mass inefficiency. Turhan pointed out that lazy bureaucrats were rewarded with outrageous benefits, while productivity declined steadily. Because of his national renown, Turhan did not need to clear publication of his articles with the newspaper's ownership. Ihsan Selimiye had been ailing for the past few years and trusted Türkoğlu implicitly. Under Turhan's direction, *Isharet* was second only to *Hürriyet* in national circulation.

Within a month of Turhan's assault on the government, hundreds of workers claimed they were "too ill" to come to work, despite a law prohibiting strikes. Turhan promised his readers he would expose massive corruption in every nationalized Turkish industry during the coming months. Each day a bold, new headline appeared in *Isharet*. Its circulation passed *Hürriyet*. Turhan's stories were picked up by the international press.

In early October, Selimiye summoned Turhan to Ankara. When Turhan arrived, he was surprised at the old man's quiet demeanor. He'd fully expected a celebration to mark *Isharet's* unparalleled success. He was even more startled when Ihsan drove them out of the city, onto the sere, dusty steppe. "Is this some sort of joke, Ihsan Bey?" Turhan asked.

"No, Turhan. A friend wants to speak with you in private."

"That would have been no problem at the hotel or anywhere else in Ankara. Why all the way out here?"

Selimiye did not respond. The car pulled up in front of a nondescript building. Turhan got out. He was startled, and not a little bit unnerved, as Ihsan immediately drove away. The sun had set. It was dim twilight. Turhan heard the unmistakable voice, raspy from what he knew was a growing overindulgence in alcohol, bidding him come inside. There were no lights on. "Sit down, Turhan. Let's talk a while."

"Why all the way out here?"

"What difference does it make?"

"None, I suppose. Is there a reason for this unusual locale?"

"There is. No one except Ihsan must know we met tonight."

"You think it's possible to keep anything secret in Turkey?"

"For your safety – for your life – it had *better* be possible."

Turhan felt cold inside. His voice remained calm. "Why would my life be in danger?"

"Your stories have created problems."

"I don't write to bring comfort to the world."

"We've discussed your philosophy before. Many times. This time, perhaps, you've overstepped your bounds."

"What do you mean, Gazi?"

"You think of me as all-powerful, Turhan. A combination of Napoleon, George Washington, perhaps even Hitler. Don't look at me like that. Weren't you the one who said 'honesty is an absolute?' Much of the world shares your view. That is not the reality. A president, a king, even a dictator, remains in power only so long as he continues to please those who exercise the *real* control."

"What are you getting at, Kemal Bey?"

"There are influential people both inside Turkey and outside our borders. Although Turkey is very proud, it is not a wealthy nation. While I'm elected by the people and the assembly, I stay in office only so long as 'they' want me there. You've made powerful enemies, Turhan."

"A journalist either kisses everyone's rear ends or he makes enemies, Gazi. That's nothing new," Turhan pointed out.

"You don't understand. These enemies want you *gone*. They feel there's no place in Turkey for investigations of the type you propose. The nation is progressing. Since they're paying for the changes, they believe they have the right to say how it runs."

"Do you agree with that, Gazi?"

"Whether I agree with it or not is irrelevant. I'm trapped. I'm the Gazi, the leader the people believe to be in complete control, but I'm powerless to oppose them."

"Then why are we here?"

"They mean to dispose of you."

"And you came to warn me?"

"Exactly. And to help you."

"How do you propose to do this?"

"You and I have been friends for eighteen years. No matter whether or not I agree with your point of view, I owe you the loyalty of that friendship."

"Gazi, I exercise the power of the largest daily newspaper in the country. All I need do is splash this story all over the front pages. I'd be protected every hour of the day."

"Just like that, eh? How influential do you think you'd continue to be once they leaked the story to *Hürriyet* about your involvement with the Agha Khorusun? Or the Agha Nikrat? Drug running has always been acceptable in Turkey, *provided* no one makes it public." Turhan paled. So it had followed him even this far. Kemal reached into a leather bag and brought forth a series of documents. "These are for you. A Turkish diplomatic passport under a different name. Addresses of trusted associates in London. My personal and confidential request that they take care of you."

"You mean, I am being banished? Exiled?"

"No, goddammit!" Atatürk roared. "*I am saving your life, you fool!* Don't you understand anything I've just said? You're supposed to be so smart. Do I have to spell it out for you? 'They' want you killed – murdered, dead, no longer alive! I have no control over them. At least you'll be safe in England."

"What about my wife?"

"As we speak, my confidants in Istanbul are talking with Sezer. She'll leave Turkey tonight, ostensibly to go to an educator's convention in London."

"What am I supposed to do in England, Gazi?"

"Survive, *Arkadash*. And Turhan?"

"Yes?"

"This meeting never took place. There must be no association of any kind between us. In two days, I will tell the 'powers' that you are not to be found, that you deserted the nation in the cowardly manner of those who spin lies."

"Gazi?"

"Yes, my friend?"

"You've been drinking more than usual, Effendim. Guard your own back door."

"You dare criticize me to my face?"

"I say this so you, too, might survive."

As Turhan left the small building, Ihsan's car reappeared. Three days later, frontier guards at the Edirne station checked the papers of a nondescript, middle-aged man who identified himself as Orfez Halip. Everything was in order. The man had first class tickets on the Simplon express from Istanbul to London. He wore the neat, pressed clothing of an international businessman. When they saw he had a red diplomatic passport, they questioned him no further, and moved on to the next passenger. No matter what the *Gazi* said, Turhan thought, it's still exile.

Less than two weeks after Turhan's departure, after more than twenty years of the closest possible collaboration with Kemal, Ismet Inönü was forced to resign as prime minister. None of the old guard remained. Kemal was entirely on his own.

12

Wien, *January 15, 1938 / **Via Diplomatic Pouch***
Personal and Confidential

Dear Turhan:

Congratulations on being hired by the B.B.C. world service! I was certain you'd land a job within a month of your arrival in London. Thank you for your congratulations as well. It feels good to be called Albay, but a full colonel is supposed to command, not simply fill the post of diplomatic attaché. I'm now beginning my third year here. Although Vienna is charming, I'm a bit nervous. You and I are both know the reason for that anxiety.

In spite of my communiqués, few people in Turkey have the least understanding about the Third Reich. The Nazis openly say the British and French have grown decadent and sick, and that Spengler's prediction of their decline was accurate. Germany is much stronger than any of us realize. It seems to have few raw materials, and hardly enough to feed its population. Yet, I've seen an aggressiveness that's frightening. I visited Berlin last month. Long lines of people waited patiently in front of food stores. There was virtually no meat, butter or fruit to be had. Our ambassador told me men's suits and women's dresses are being made out of wood pulp. Gasoline and rubber are manufactured from coal and lime. The Reichsmark is not backed by gold or anything else. It's difficult to see how the Germans are able to import anything.

Yet, Germany is making feverish efforts to become self-sufficient. I believe the Reich is preparing for total war. Their four year plan is deadly serious. Despite their apparent dislike of Nazism, the vast majority of German people believe in Hitler and stand behind him all the way. The Führer prattles on about peace to high-ranking foreign visitors. He tells Londoners, Parisians or New Yorkers that he was in the trenches during the last war, that he knows what war is, and that he'd never dream of condemning mankind to a repeat of the Great War. Yet two hundred thousand gather in the Sportpalast and sing the Nazi marching song that goes, "Today we own Germany, tomorrow the whole world!"

Have you heard anything more about the Gazi's illness? Obviously I couch this phrase very carefully, in the event someone reads this letter before it gets to you. May Allah protect his footsteps, and all that. Funny, if Kemal saw this letter, he'd laugh out loud. He never cared a whit for the religious state. He's always wanted to be a western-style leader. Enough, arkadash. You get my drift.

Schuschnigg, the Austrian Chancellor, seems in control for the present, but no one knows how long it will be before the Nazis look toward their southern flank. After all, the Führer was born in Austria. He's made noises about a Greater Reich, since Dolfuss, the previous chancellor, was assassinated four years ago. The "late midget," as they're calling him, may unwittingly have set things up for Hitler by destroying the Social Democrats.

Two weeks ago, I returned to Vienna, city of Strauss and gemütlichkeit, charm and intelligence. What a difference between the Prussians and the Austrians! Even though Vienna is almost as poor as Berlin and there are beggars on every corner, I love the baroque architecture, the music, and the soft, lilting Viennese accent. There's a great deal of anti-Jewish feeling here. I'm told this city has been heavily anti-Semitic since the last century, though many of the men who made Vienna a world center – Mahler, Freud, Einstein, Karoly – are Jewish. Vienna's anti-Semitism plays into the Nazis's hands. Several Jews are trying desperately to get out of Austria, but many more are staying, convinced they'll ride out any troubles. I think they're incredibly naïve and shortsighted.

Two nights ago, at an embassy function, I met two German Jews who asked about you, Bernhard and Rachela Friedman. He's a corpulent fellow who maintains that money will always buy safety. His wife is a pretty little woman who sees reality much more clearly than her husband.

Aysheh asked to be remembered to you. I confide only to you that her gaiety seems forced and artificial. I suspect she may be drinking more than is good for her, perhaps from boredom, or because I travel quite a bit while she remains here. I must have words with her, although I don't quite know how to broach the subject.

Once again, congratulations. My fondest regards to Sezer. Nadji

London, February 16, 1938
Extremely confidential / Via Diplomatic Pouch

Dear Nadji:

What in the hell is going on there?

I found out from very reliable sources that Chancellor Schuschnigg had a secret meeting with Hitler at Berchtesgaden and that the Führer demanded Schuschnigg appoint several Nazis to the Austrian cabinet, grant amnesty for all Nazi prisoners, and restore the political rights of the Nazi party, or else the Reichswehr would invade Austria. I've been told there is a new Minister of the Interior and an amnesty has been announced. ???? -Turhan

On Friday, March 11, the sun was out. Spring was in the air. The overnight train from Belgrade arrived at the *Sudbahnhof* shortly after eight thirty that morning. Nadji's driver picked him up, then drove toward the colonel's apartment. When the car reached Mariahilferstrasse, Vienna's main shopping thoroughfare, Nadji was surprised to find the usually clean streets littered with paper. He cracked open the car's window and heard a buzzing sound. As he looked up, he saw a pair of airplanes dropping leaflets about the capital.

"Plebiscite," the driver remarked. "The one Schuschnigg ordered."

Nadji didn't press the issue. It would not look good for him to appear uninformed. When he arrived home, he went into the bedroom. Aysheh was asleep. Damn, she was still a beautiful woman! He felt like slipping in beside her. His eyes strayed to the nightstand. He saw a half-consumed bottle of gin. *Damn!* Not again! If only she hadn't lost the baby last year! It had gotten worse since then. Much worse. He closed the door quietly. When he returned to the front room, he saw several days' worth of newspapers stacked haphazardly on the coffee table. He ignored the disarray and the mildly alcoholic smell of the place. He thumbed through the papers. The March 10 edition of the Tageblatt blared, "*PLEBISCITE!*"

Nadji read the news under the banner headline. Last Wednesday night, Chancellor Schuschnigg, speaking at Innsbruck, had ordered a national vote to take place March 13. The single question to be determined was, "Are you for an *independent*, social, Christian, united

Austria? *Ja oder Nein.*" Schuschnigg announced he had the support of the workers and was certain he would win in the coming vote.

Maybe, maybe not, Nadji thought. He doubted that Hitler would accept an affirmative vote. The Führer had already broken a dozen solemn promises, pledges and treaties to everyone else. Why should the vote of a weak Austrian state make a difference? The most current newspapers were full of information about the plebiscite, exhorting the Viennese to vote, to protect their way of life. Nadji reflected back to the time he'd first come to Vienna. How much of that way of life had evaporated!

There was no way he could make a decent breakfast without awakening Aysheh, so he walked several blocks to the embassy, where he had a small meal. His mood throughout the day was grim. Sooner or later, he'd have to face the reality that his lovely wife was drunk more often than she was sober. He'd become upset, then repulsed by her inebriated advances. There'd been ugly arguments that had become more frequent since her miscarriage – angry, embittered words on both sides that had started to rip the fabric of their marriage. He still loved her. An affair was unthinkable for many reasons. First, he had no desire for anyone other than his wife, provided she was sober. Second, he was an *Albay*, a full colonel, at thirty-five. Clearly he was destined for bigger things. To risk any hint of impropriety would be to lose the general's stars he'd aspired to for as long as he could remember. Third … well, there really was no third. He loved her, but how long could love withstand the continuous pummeling by such rapidly escalating discomfort?

Shortly before five in the afternoon, Nadji heard a commotion outside the embassy. When he went out to investigate, there were more than a thousand people wearing swastika arm bands. Since the police appeared to be in control, he thought nothing of it and returned to his office. An hour later, a mob of five thousand Nazis swarmed up the street. Nadji felt a chill reminiscent of what he'd experienced a few months ago when he'd attended a mass rally in Berlin. People in the crowd appeared glassy eyed and were shouting, *"Sieg Heil! Sieg Heil! Heil Hitler! Schuschnigg 'Raus! Ein Volk, Ein Reich, Ein Führer*!! The police looked on, doing nothing. Nadji attempted to call home to find out if Aysheh was all right. The lines were not working. He decided to walk to his apartment. When he went outside to ask a policeman what had happened, the officer answered, "The plebiscite has been called off." He returned to the embassy and tuned in Radio Wien. Within moments, the Strauss waltz playing on the air was interrupted by a male voice. *"Achtung!* Attention! In a few minutes you will hear an important announcement." Chancellor Schuschnigg came on the radio without introduction. His voice almost broke several times during the brief speech, but he somehow held it under control.

"My fellow citizens. This day has placed us in a tragic and decisive situation. The German government today handed President Miklas an ultimatum, ordering him to nominate a chancellor and cabinet designated by the Reich. If he did not do so within twelve hours, German troops would invade Austria. I declare before the world that German reports concerning disorders by the workers, the shedding of streams of blood, and the creation of a situation beyond the control of the Austrian government are all lies. Austria has yielded to force. We are not prepared, even in this terrible situation, to shed blood. It is with a broken heart that we have decided to advise our troops to stand down. I take leave of the Austrian people with a word of farewell uttered from the depth of my heart. May God protect Austria."

The radio played a recording of a tune originally composed by Josef Haydn, which now, given the words *"Deutschland über Alles,"* had a sinister ring. A little later, Doctor Seyss-Inquart, the new Interior

Minister, came on the air. He announced that he considered himself responsible for order, and commanded the Austrian army not to offer resistance. Nadji stared at the receiver dumbfounded. *Resistance to what?* Schuschnigg had said the German ultimatum was capitulation *or* invasion. Had the Nazis already broken the terms of their own ultimatum?

Nadji attempted to call his apartment again. The lines were still down. He'd have to fight his way through the crowds. As he moved toward the *Kärntnerstrasse,* there were mobs everywhere on the street, singing Nazi songs. The few policemen who stood around now wore swastika arm bands. On the main street, Nadji was startled to see a vaguely familiar figure. He raked his mind to try to recall where he'd seen the face before. Abbas? Abbas Hükümdar? No, it couldn't be. Not in Vienna. He must be imagining things. The other man took no notice of him.

Nadji worked his way toward the *Graben.* He saw young toughs, heaving bricks through the windows of Jewish shops. The crowd applauded their efforts and hurled stones and garbage through the broken plate glass. In less than an hour, Vienna had been transformed into a Reich city. The red, white and black swastika flag draped every public building. It took Nadji two hours to walk home.

When he got there, he saw slices of cold *wurst* on a plate, an uncut loaf of pumpernickel bread, and a half-empty bottle of wine on a counter in the kitchen. Aysheh sat on a chair nearby, her nightdress askew, staring coldly out the window. "Your lovely Wien," she remarked, dully. "City of Strauss and *Sachertorte, kaffee mit schlag,* refinement and taste. City of death!" she said, angrily turning toward him. "You brought me here, you bastard! You leave me alone day and night while you go about your business, and travel to foreign countries. The great *Albay,* soon-to-be *Pasha.* And you can't even make love to your wife anymore!"

"You've been drinking again, Aysheh," he said tightly.

"What if I have? Do you even give a damn? I'm bored in this hellhole and I'm scared out of my mind. I can't go out anymore. I'm a foreigner, a Turk, treated like the Jews they're attacking every day. What do you expect, Nadji? That I'll sit here all day, the dutiful wife, waiting patiently for her man to come home and grace her with his presence? I want to go home, Nadji! I want a husband and babies. You promised me a baby last year, and the year before that, and the year before that. Are you afraid that because I've lost one, I can't give you healthy sons? What in the name of Allah do you want from me?"

She staggered drunkenly to her feet and collapsed against him. He took her in his arms. For an instant, he was stirred. Then he smelled the alcohol, and saw that her beautiful grey-violet eyes were unseeing. He lifted her small body and gently carried her into the bedroom. He covered the half-clothed form, returned to the living room, and made himself a bed on the sofa.

"You're sure no one noticed you're in Vienna?"

"Positive, Papa."

"What good luck that Heydrich alerted you it was going to happen. When are you coming back?"

"Two days. The Simplon."

"You don't feel like fooling around up in Berlin? After all, my boy, you've earned a bit of a holiday."

"No, thank you Mister Minister. My God, it's hard to believe I now occupy the position you did when you first proposed I marry Mina. I have you to thank for everything, Papa."

"Look, Abbas, one hand washes the other. Your performance – your superb investigation and disclosure of my predecessor's secret letters to the World Jewish Organization promising them aid, violating the very basis of Turkish neutrality – was a key factor in my own promotion."

"Slowly we purify our own, eh, sir?"

"Indeed. Both your names fit you well, son. 'Clever Abbas' from the early days. And if I have any say, Hükümdar the prince will one day succeed to the throne of the Interior Ministry."

13

March 12, 1938
Via Diplomatic Pouch
To: Turkish Ambassador, London, England
From: Ankara / Foreign Ministry

Extremely Urgent/Classified: Turkish Ambassador's Eyes Only.

Your Excellency:

Gazi Mustafa Kemal Atatürk is most seriously ill. The diagnosis is cirrhosis of the liver. The prognosis is very grave. The yacht Savarona *in the London dockyards is for sale. The Grand National Assembly requests you extend the greatest courtesy and assistance to Ekrem Küchük, who will negotiate to purchase this yacht for the Gazi's use. Your staff is to be advised only that Kemal is exhausted from overwork. It is anticipated that Atatürk will spend the time he has remaining aboard the boat. May Allah Protect Turkey.*

14

Spring of 1938 was a dismal time for the Jews of Vienna. In making a "routine audit" of the records of the Jewish community organization, Nazi occupiers found receipts showing that the Jews had spent 550,000 *reichsmarks* to support Schuschnigg's toppled government. The new rulers of *Östmark* promptly levied a fine of 550,000 *reichsmarks* against the entire Jewish population and threatened to seize every piece of *Juden*-owned property in Austria if the fine was not paid immediately. The new government forced Jewish work crews to clean Vienna's streets, on their hands and knees, using toothbrushes. The *Aryan* population thought it a grand game to defecate or pour garbage in the streets, just after they'd been cleaned, so that the hated Jews would have to go back and do it again.

Often Jews were rounded up and made to stand all day in a fenced-in school yard as they waited their turn to proceed to a "work detail." There were no toilet facilities. They were given no opportunity to relieve themselves. Many men simply urinated in their pants, and prayed that not so much as one drop would spill on the ground. If Nazi overlords saw such spoliation of so much as one inch of precious Reich land, the offending Jew was told to lick the urine dry or suffer merciless whippings until he could no longer stand.

Jewish children, long barred from attending public schools, continued their studies in crowded, stuffy Talmud-Torahs within the synagogues. When they were prohibited from using these temples, they attended classes in the cellars of private homes. Viennese authorities raided these schools an average of twice a week. Jewish children were marched down to the city's commercial streets. The Nazis were meticulous record-keepers and knew which *Jude* owned a particular business. Each son or daughter was made to paint, "This business is owned by a filthy Jew, an enemy of the State and a Christ killer. Please do not patronize this store," and sign his or her name below, on the window of a shop owned by that child's parents. Friedman's Department Store in Vienna was open only two hours a day. Bernhard hired armed guards. The windows were perpetually covered by iron bars. This did not stop Nazi thugs from bursting into the store one day, and spraying sulfuric acid over everything in the place.

During the last weeks of summer, 1938, Hitler and Neville Chamberlain, the British Prime Minister met at Munich and engaged in the most serious talks since the Chancellor had taken over control of the Reich. The *Völkischer Beobachter* screamed, *"WOMEN AND CHILDREN MOWED DOWN BY CZECH ARMORED CARS!"*, *"EXTORTION, PLUNDERING, SHOOTING – CZECH TERROR IN SUDETEN GERMAN LAND GROWS WORSE EACH DAY!"*

At thirty minutes after midnight, September 30, 1938, less than twenty-four hours before the Führer's threatened commencement of the great European war, Hitler, Mussolini, Chamberlain, and Daladier of France signed a pact turning the Sudetenland over to Germany. That night, to the sound of English crowds shouting, "Good old Neville" and singing "For he's a jolly good fellow," the British Prime

Minister announced from the balcony of 10 Downing Street that he had achieved "peace with honor for our time."

Early in November, a Jewish exile shot Ernst vom Rath, a legation secretary in the German embassy in Paris. Within twenty-four hours, on November 9, 1938, synagogues went up in flames all over Germany. Jewish homes were devastated, stores pillaged and destroyed. More than a hundred people were killed. Twenty-five thousand were arrested. By the next sunset, *Kristallnacht* – Crystal Night – had spread to Vienna. Four of the five large synagogues in the city, including the Turkish Synagogue at 22 Zirkusgasse in the Third *Bezirk*, were burned to the ground. Not one major Jewish-owned business was left intact. Viennese newspapers demanded a final solution to the Jewish problem.

Austrian citizens, bearing yellow passports on which had been stamped the middle name *Israel* for males, *Sarah* for females, waited in lines at every major embassy in the city. Some were lucky and went to less desirable consular offices for a visa – Poland, Rumania, even the Soviet Union. More desirable countries set up "quotas." Turkish Jews had been established in Vienna for two hundred years, but they'd retained their national identity. Now, they sought exit from the greater Reich en masse. But on the day after Reich's Kristallnacht and for several days thereafter, they found the Turkish embassy doors barred and the consular offices closed. For Turkey had suffered its own tragedy, and the rest of the world must be ignored.

15

On November 11, 1938, over the sound of Big Ben's chimes, a baritone voice announced, "This is London calling, the world service of the B.B.C." We interrupt our regularly-scheduled broadcast for a special report from Turhan Türkoğlu in Istanbul, Turkey."

Turhan's voice, which had become the most widely listened-to by Turks throughout the world, was subdued. He spoke in Turkish, then in accented, but excellent English. "Good evening, my friends. But it is not a good evening in Istanbul, for Turkey grieves bitterly this night. The man who brought our motherland forward five centuries within fifteen years, is dead.

"Many condemned Mustafa Kemal Atatürk as a dictator, the man who would not only be king, but who would be God as well. A year ago, I was sent into exile in England. At his instigation, I escaped those who would have murdered me. He was my friend. He will always be my friend. It is because of Kemal Atatürk that you hear my voice today. If, during this broadcast, I break down and weep, bear with me, for the tears must come if there is to be a cleansing.

"Eight months ago, the *Gazi* – the conqueror of the infidels – realized he was dying. Last March, the Republic purchased the yacht *Savarona* for the President. When it arrived in Istanbul, Kemal remarked, 'I have waited for this yacht like a child expecting a toy. Is she to become my grave?' The words were tragically prophetic.

"Dr. Fissinger, the specialist flown here from Paris, remained at the *Gazi's* side for three months. Only once during that time did he leave. That was when Atatürk ordered him to examine Ismet Inönü, the *Gazi's* closest friend, in Ankara. Ismet, gravely ill with diabetes, could not visit the president.

"During his last months, Kemal's constant companion was a young child, Ülkü, the last of his adopted daughters. She amused him for hours with her childish games. He often said she was the only one who always told him the truth. By September 5, Atatürk knew the end was near. He signed a will leaving his estate to the people of Turkey.

"I am broadcasting from a studio near the grounds of the Dolmabahche Palace. For my English language listeners, the word conjures up dolma, or stuffed grape leaves. The term is accurate. Dolmabahche is not like the spare Topkapı Palace, which the Ottoman sultans inhabited for hundreds of years. Dolmabahche was built seventy-five years ago, when the Ottoman Empire was called 'the sick man of Europe,' to show that Turkey could compete with any castle built in the west. The palace sits astride the Bosphorous. To many, it is a gaudy, pretentious bastion of the most grandiose poor taste imaginable. But I spent many years in the shadow of its gates, and I find it magnificent. To enter the grand hall and see the three-story high crystal chandelier, to walk the flights of a wide crystal staircase, and to peek into the harem rooms, are things I can never forget.

"After he executed his will, Kemal was moved from the *Savarona* to Dolmabahche, where he spent his last days. Several weeks ago, he knew the republic's fifteenth anniversary was approaching. More than anything he wanted to go to Ankara and speak to the Grand National

Assembly. But twelve days before the celebration, the president fell into a coma. He recovered two days later and stubbornly prepared the draft of his speech. He ordered that a special lift be installed in the stadium, to take him to his box, and that a rostrum be constructed in the assembly, from which he could lean back, half sitting, but seem to be standing. It was to no avail. The doctors said the journey by train might be fatal, that he was too weak to walk at all.

"On October 29, 1938, on the fifteenth anniversary of the republic, a group of cadets from Kuleli Military School passed in front of Dolmabahche in a boat, shouting in unison, 'We want to see Atatürk!' Somehow, Mustafa Kemal made it to a window and waved weakly at the cadets. They roared his name, over and over. They sang the Turkish national anthem to him. Some of them jumped into the water in their uniforms, and swam toward the palace, to see him more closely. That night, the *Gazi* watched fireworks bursting throughout the city. Next morning, he privately told his aides he wanted Ismet Inönü to succeed him to the presidency."

Turhan's voice sounded choked, as he continued. "On November 6, Atatürk got up for the last time. The next day, the doctors drew off a large quantity of fluid. Afterward, the *Gazi* had a craving for an artichoke. They were out of season, but a consignment was flown by military aircraft to Istanbul. When the artichoke came, Atatürk could not eat it. Not long afterward, he had a painful seizure, murmured 'Good-bye,' and fell into his last coma.

"At 9:07 on the morning of November 10, 1938, the *Gazi* passed away. Clocks stopped all over Turkey. Istanbul was stunned into silence. For the next three days, a million people filed endlessly, reverently past the flag-draped, ebony coffin, bowing silently, whispering prayers, softly murmuring '*Ata, ata*' for their father, who was dead. On the third night, his coffin was borne on a gun carriage, drawn by soldiers in slow procession, to the wharf below Topkapı. An officer marched behind the carriage, carrying a solitary medal, that of the War of Independence, on a red velvet cushion. As they crossed Galata Bridge, the Turkish military band played Chopin's Funeral March, and a torpedo boat carried the coffin to the packet steamer *Yavuz*. For an instant, today's problems were put aside. Ships from Germany, Russia, England, France, Italy, Greece, and the United States, even H.M.S. Malaya, which had carried the last sultan into exile, slowly escorted the Yavuz out of the Bosphorous, into the Sea of Marmara. The coffin will travel to Ankara in the presidential train, where the *Gazi's* mortal remains will be buried.

"The father of Turkey is dead. The Turkish nation is bereft of its soul. We weep unashamedly, with a broken heart. It was my privilege to live during the years of Mustafa Kemal. It was my greater honor to call him my friend. Now he is gone. There is an emptiness in all of us, for there will never be another such as he. *Mashallah*. With a grief so great I can speak no more, I bid you farewell from Istanbul, the Turkish republic."

16

On December 29, 1938, the Turkish embassy in Vienna held a small party in Nadji's honor. After three years of honorable service, he was returning to Istanbul on assignment to the Turkish military security office. Nadji felt mixed emotions. He was relieved to be departing the cold, stifling atmosphere of a greater Reich state, but dreaded the confrontation that faced him in Turkey. Six months ago, he'd refused Aysheh's demand that he request compassionate reassignment. She'd left Vienna to take up residence in Ankara. A month ago, some friends advised him that she'd been seen in the company of the vice minister for public transportation. Initially, he'd been sickened by the thought of his beautiful wife in the arms of another man. He contemplated flying to Ankara to demand the death, or, at the very least, the public dishonor of the immoral couple. In the end, he'd remained in Vienna, burying his misery in the conduct of business.

Nadji noticed the Friedmans on the periphery of the small crowd. They appeared desperately to be signaling him. Bernhard Friedman was almost unrecognizable. He'd lost fifty pounds. His eyes were sunken, red-rimmed. He had a haunted, hopeless look. "I gather you know what's happened to us," he began. "We've lost almost everything. I fear we'll shortly be receiving documents advising that we're being 'resettled.' Colonel, I beg you, if you can't help me, can you at least help Rachela?"

Nadji winced. He'd heard of these "resettlement" camps before. The tales were veiled but sinister. He looked sympathetically at these people who'd done no wrong. Tiny Rachela was thinner than he'd remembered. "Have you any contacts in Turkey? Anyone who would sponsor you?"

"Turhan Türkoğlu," Bernhard answered immediately. "He and his wife met us in Berlin and had dinner in our home."

"Unfortunately, Turhan was banished by Atatürk in 1937. Although there's talk that Ismet İnönü, who's now president, wants to grant him complete amnesty, that hasn't gone through yet. Do you have any friends in the Turkish Jewish community?"

"The *khakham*, the Jewish spiritual leader in Istanbul."

"Good. I'll speak with our consulate this evening."

"How long would it take?"

"You could be in Istanbul within a month."

"But you'll be gone."

"I'll stay in touch." As he walked back to the center of the party, Nadji's eye caught that of another man, a few years older than himself.

"Congratulations, *Albay*. Looks like you've done well for yourself even if you chose to reject the Brotherhood."

"Mister Minister," Nadji said politely, deferring to Abbas' rank of Deputy Interior Minister. "Aren't you a bit far from home?"

"Protecting investments, Colonel. You know, you really shouldn't be seen talking intimately with Jews. They're little more than the walking dead."

"I happen to believe otherwise, Minister Hükümdar, even though that puts us on opposite sides of the fence."

"I'd guard my fences were I you, Colonel. After all, your wife's learned where power lies. Perhaps you might pay heed to lessons you could learn from her."

"Listen, you bastard," Nadji said softly, under his breath. "Your department knows all the dirt about everyone who's anyone. At least her "friend" is not an anti-Semite."

"I'd say 'touché,' but an imperious tone does not befit a cuckold," Abbas rejoined. "I advise you for your own good, regardless what you might think of me. Or are you no longer interested in becoming a pasha?" The Deputy Minister bowed his head slightly, turned on his heel, and walked briskly away.

Next day, Nadji left for home. He located the Jewish community leader, and expedited all necessary papers, which he then arranged to have shipped to Vienna by diplomatic courier. At his request, the embassy dispatched a messenger to personally deliver the documents to the Friedman's home, within three weeks of the morning he left Vienna. When the messenger knocked on the door, he was greeted by a heavyset, sad-eyed woman. "I'm so sorry," she responded. "The Friedmans have been resettled. I'm afraid I don't have a forwarding address for them."

17

"Turhan, Sezer, I thought you'd stay in England for the duration." The three of them were sitting around Halide's dinner table, having just enjoyed an elegant supper, which their hostess had prepared.

"Thank you, no," Turhan responded. "My job will be to keep Turkey out of this war if I can. By articles, by broadcasts, by anything that will work."

"So you've made your peace with our government's industrial elite?"

"Let's just say we're in an uneasy truce," he said, chuckling. "They've agreed to let me stay in Turkey as long as I 'behave.'"

"You'll be in Istanbul?"

"No," said Sezer, squeezing her husband's hand. It was obvious that whatever had separated them in the past was buried in the past, and they now seemed as happy and content with one another as any married couple can be. "He'll be in Ankara as Editor-in-Chief of *Isharet* and he'll be broadcasting daily from radio house."

"I'm impressed." She smiled. "I'm so pleased you're back, Sezer. You were my first recruiter and you're still the best."

PART FOUR: HEROES 1928–1937 – CHAPTER 17   233

"What do you mean?" Turhan said. "Yujel Orhan Teachers' College is internationally famous. Students are churning up the Bosphorous to get in. I understand the government is underwriting expenses and you're filled with applicants for years to come."

"I'm not so interested in getting students. I need teachers."

"You've no shortage of them either, from what I hear."

"Anyone can find a student. Anyone can find a teacher. But I'm looking for those very special villagers, men and women, who will learn the language and who won't lose their identity with the village. I want the Sezers of Turkey, who'll return not only with the new language, but with the old folk tales."

"So you're sending my wife out into the hinterlands once again?" he said.

"Ankara's hardly the hinterlands, and besides you'll be there. I need a representative in the capital whom I can trust completely."

"Have the two of you discussed this already?"

"Of course, darling." Sezer reached over and pinched his cheek. "I really would like one last chance to work before we start our family. After all, you're the one who kept saying we must wait for a child until we got back to Turkey."

"Will Sezer have to travel?" Turhan asked.

"Very little," Halide answered. "Once or twice a year, she'll go east, simply to supervise what's going on, and she'll travel to Istanbul as often as she wants to."

"Why, you stingy woman," Turhan said, grinning broadly. "Is my wife expected to work for slave wages or not? I've heard the reason you're so wealthy is that you have the first *kurush* you ever earned in Turkey – and all the rest of them as well."

"I'll have you know, Sir, your wife will be earning as much as the sultans of old."

"That's wonderful. The sultans received no salary."

"Very perceptive, my friend."

"You mean?"

"Listen, 'Voice of Turkey.' You're not starving. A wife is entitled to depend on her husband for support."

As they snuggled together in bed, Sezer sighed happily. "If someone had told me five years ago that we'd be this happy, I would have wept unbelieving tears."

"Well, it just goes to show that even an old ox like me can learn what's truly important."

"Old ox? You're only forty-one. That's hardly someone who's a candidate for the graveyard. How do you feel about becoming a father for the first time?"

"Probably a lot more nervous than you." He reached over and touched the swell of her stomach gently. "Hey, I just felt him kick!"

"What makes you think it's a 'him'? Haven't I taught you yet that women have an equal opportunity." She shoved him gently, then put her arm around his shoulder.

"More stuff you learned from Halide?"

"No. More stuff I've learned from life."

"How do you think you'll be able to adjust to home life when the baby comes?"

"Easy," she chided. "I'll do what Turkish village women have done for centuries. I've already bought two 'baby drains,' she said." In

Turkish villages throughout the land, women swaddled their babes in towels and inserted wooden tubes in the areas where the little ones would be expected to evacuate. They would then strap the babies on their backs and work most of the day with the youngsters sleeping, voiding, or gurgling as the need arose.

"You're joking," Turhan said half-seriously.

"Maybe. But I'll probably wait until our baby – son or daughter – is five or so before I go back to work."

"You want to stop at one?"

"That depends. It feels so good to try to make them."

She snuggled against his back and soon they drifted off to sleep, completely satisfied with one another.

As winter covered the capital with snow, Turhan told Sezer, "I've got to go to London for two weeks. The BBC's been pressing. The Turkish embassy asked me to go as a favor to them."

"Turhan, I'm worried for your safety. Read your own articles! Russia invaded Finland and the Germans scuttled their supposedly invincible pocket battleship, the *Graf Spee* off Uruguay. This is serious war. You're rushing off to the middle of it."

"Come with me, then."

"No," she said. "I don't want to go. I don't think you should, either. I went with you before. This time I think you should stay with me."

"It's only for two weeks."

"In the middle of winter, no less."

"But I'll need warming up when I get back."

She glared at him, then softened. "As long as you refuse the loving invitation of your wife and seem bent on going into the middle of the most dangerous place on earth, make sure you wear your hat and galoshes, and try to dress like a westerner instead of a Turkish peasant."

"What will you do while I'm gone?"

"Halide's wanted me to go east for two months now. There's no reason to stay in Ankara with you gone."

"I thought you were going to postpone the trip 'til spring. The roads are atrocious once you get beyond Sivas."

"It's probably the last time I'll be able to travel before the baby comes. Besides, what else have I got to do while my man is gone? Sit around Ankara and watch the snow as it turns black with soot?"

"Why not wait and we'll go together in spring?"

"With a seven months' growth of belly? Turhan, my dear, I think I'll go east, even if only as far as Erzinjan."

"I'd rather you wouldn't during the winter. You never can tell what might happen out there," Turhan said.

"If you stayed here, I wouldn't go. Why don't we both just stay in Ankara?"

"That's not my way, Sezer."

"Be careful, then."

"You too, my love."

Turhan had been in London less than a week when he received an emergency call from Istanbul. He recognized the voice, but the static on the line made comprehension difficult. "Speak up, Halide. The connection is very bad. I can't hear you."

"Turhan, you must come home at once!"

"Why, is something wrong?"

"You haven't heard the news?"

"What, about the war?"

"No. There's been an earthquake in Erzinjan. The initial reports say forty-five thousand have been killed."

"Forty-five *THOUSAND*? There haven't been that many people killed in Europe since the end of the Great War! Wait a minute, Halide. Sezer was going to be in Erzinjan this week… Oh, my God! Are you saying?…"

"Turhan, my dear, dear Turhan," Halide said, her voice breaking. "They found her body in the ruins this morning."

HUGO N. GERSTL COLLECTION

See below some of Pangæa Publishing Group's
bestsellers by the same author:

Do not miss them on your shelf!

For Hugo N. Gerstl's complete novels list and descriptions,
go to www.HugoGerstl.com

PANGÆA PUBLISHING GROUP
25579 Carmel Knolls Drive
Carmel, CA 93923
Email: info@pangaeapublishing.com

PANGÆA

Printed in Great Britain
by Amazon